Rachel

K. B. Sykes Publishing

North East Lincolnshire, England

www.kbsykespublishing.co.uk

1

ISBN: 978-0-9556761-2-3

Chapter 1

The sun streamed in through the pale curtains and streaked its early morning brightness across two slumbering bodies in an unmade bed. Rachel murmured to herself as she forced her eyes open, writhed slowly and slid her way to the edge of the mattress. The covered body behind her stirred beneath the duvet with a muffled grumble. She stood up quietly and cautiously, careful not to move her head too much or cause any further aches and pains by moving too quickly. Her mouth felt dry and her eyes were sensitive to the light. She rubbed her forehead softly and gently combed her fingers through her long, blonde hair. Motionless for a moment, she drew a slow, deep breath and walked quietly through to the en-suite shower room, collecting her handbag from the bedside table as she passed. The door clicked quietly closed behind her and she turned to face the mirror above the hand basin. Her mirror image seemed to be wavering, as if distorted by rising heat.

"Bastard must have spiked me!" she whispered to her reflection as she tried to focus.

She splashed cold water over her face and drank a couple of gulps from her hands. Immediately, a wave of welcome relief as the cold water cooled and refreshed her from inside swept through her. Gasping for further gratification, she cupped her hand beneath the tap and drank more. After several mouthfuls and a relieved exhalation of satisfaction, she stood up and took a few deep breaths. She paused and tried to steady her grip on reality. Determined to gather her thoughts, she stared into her reflection, which had now become still and then attempted to read the inscription beneath the small Hotel logo on the mirror. She scrunched her eyes and tried hard to focus on the Latin phrase, but her early morning suffering had not quite subsided and would not allow her to understand what she was looking at. Slightly despondent following her efforts, she squatted above the toilet and retrieved her contraceptive cap that she had been wearing all night. With a disgusted look on her face and a dirty feeling inside, she wrapped it securely in a piece of tissue and dropped it in the sanitary bin next to the toilet. How she wished she could dispose of her sordid life in such a simple way.

Thinking the shower would have been too loud and may have woken her companion; she stepped gingerly into the bath and washed her naked body straight from the tap, delicately from top to bottom. On the shelf by the shower, she found a complimentary sponge and a bottle of soap. The soap was surprisingly luxurious, which was not at all what she expected, although the sponge itself was slightly crisp. The water was cool and left her covered with goose bumps but a brisk rub down with the towel from the rail soon warmed her.

Face to face with herself in the mirror again, she looked deep into her green eyes. Shaking her head slowly as she patted herself dry, she flicked her hair down across her field of vision and diligently snapped off a few split ends. She brushed her hair back off her face and tied it in a loose ponytail, then leaned forward to get a clearer view of her complexion. Pulling her skin taught around her eyes, she applied her expensive moisturiser, the only brand she had any faith in, with a delicate touch and a sense of satisfaction. Content that she had warded off the ageing process for another day, she quietly returned to the bedroom.

Struggling with her feelings, she took a clean pair of knickers from her handbag and began to dress. Determined not to attract the attention of her sleeping companion, she slowly, quietly, slipped her long shapely legs into her tight blue jeans. With every sound that might prove faintly audible, she froze, grimaced and hoped that her companion would sleep through the mild disturbance. She pulled a loose cotton blouse with the buttons still fastened over her head, straightened it out and flicked her long hair out of her collar. Standing straight with her shoulders back in front of a long mirror, she adjusted her breasts with her cupped hands until she was satisfied that they looked even. As she turned her back to the mirror to admire herself over her shoulder, she smoothed out the seat of her jeans and felt her buttocks.

"Still got that!" she whispered with a smile, "What a fantastic arse!"

She turned to survey the bedroom and rescue her belongings from various points across the floor. A tattooed arm and an occasional grunt were the only signs of life coming from beneath the duvet, pulled into a heap on one side of the bed. Rachel began to feel confident about the level of background noise she could get away with and began to relax a little. From under the bed she retrieved her shoe; the other was across the room by a chair. She decided against putting them on now and instead carried them by the straps. Gathering up her handbag and jacket from the chair by the dressing table, she saw her white lace bra by the foot of the bed.

"We'll call that a keepsake shall we honey?" she whispered as she threw it lightly onto the piled up duvet.

Just then, the pile moved and a string of audible groans, closely resembling words, emanated from within. Rachel froze. The tattooed arm moved. Rachel flinched. With the clacking sound of smacking lips, the duvet stilled and the sounds faded to silence. When she became comfortable in the quiet and reassured herself that he was still sleeping, she leaned over to the bedside table. Without a hint of guilt or conscience, she carefully picked up a wallet, a gold watch and a bunch of keys. Tiptoeing almost comically, she sneaked out of the room and into the hall.

The hallway was short and repetitive. All the doors along both walls were exact replicas of each other with the same floral design on each of the number plaques. Incorporated into the wallpaper and decorated with swirling flowers, the logo with the confusing slogan taunted Rachel. The pattern on the carpet seemed to fractalise down the length of the hall, mirrored from ceiling to floor at both ends, adding a perception of length. An infinite number of mirror images of Rachel, surrounded by the floral swirl, faded off into the distance and conflicted with her hangover.

She felt light-headed and had to pause for a moment to steady herself; with one hand against the wall, she slipped her shoes on before she walked briskly towards the lift. She found it easier and less dizzying to keep her eyes on the carpet and not look up into the mirror. The doors slid back just as she approached the lift and a young maid pushing a trolley laden with bed linen appeared with a polite smile.

"Morning," they whispered to each other, almost in unison.

Rachel reached out and pressed the 'G' button on the panel that immediately illuminated green. An unexpected, polite, recorded voice of a woman told her to mind the doors and repeated that she was going to the ground level. The doors slid closed and the lift jolted into a smooth descent, which made Rachel's stomach spin as if she had driven too quickly over a hump-backed bridge.

"Never again, Rachel. Don't do this again," she thought to herself, desperately trying to convince herself that she wanted out.

In need of stability, she grabbed the handrail on the mirrored back wall. Unwavering, she took the opportunity to put on a quick, though precise and affectionately applied, dab of make-up before she turned her attention to the possessions she had taken from the room. She looked thoughtfully at the watch with her head tilted to one side,

"Fake," she said to herself quietly, "but a good one!" and then slid it into her jacket pocket.

She opened the wallet, removed the cash, counted quickly and smiled.

"£155? Not bad!" she thought.

Thumbing through the credit and debit cards, she decided she didn't want them. Suddenly, the polite voice startled her again as it announced that the lift had arrived at her destination, which it did with a slight bump, and Rachel stepped out into the reception area. Sneakily, she dropped the wallet and the unwanted cards in a black rubbish bag on a service trolley outside the lift as the member of cleaning staff had her back turned. With the cash slid neatly into her back pocket, she walked through the broad foyer.

The early morning bustle was another two hours away at least and there were no other guests in view. Only smartly dressed members of staff walked briskly in and then out of view, preparing for another busy day at the Grande Hotel Victoria.

Rachel took the rear exit to the car park and held aloft the bunch of keys. She pressed the little button with her thumb as she pointed her fist in the general direction of the cars. A Mercedes convertible caught her attention as she looked down the rows of vehicles. Her reflection in the window offered her another opportunity to check her hair. A silver Rolls Royce took pride of place in a large 'reserved' bay next to a vintage, metallic blue Aston Martin in a similar bay. Doubtfully pointing the keys at the executive cars she wished for a response from the lights but got nothing. With a sigh and a shrug of her shoulders, she continued walking down the aisles of cars. She pressed the button intermittently until she saw the flash of orange indicators in the distance, accompanied by a double click, which quickened her pace to a silver Lexus LS460.

"Smart," she said, "but I'd rather have had the Martin!"

Smoothing herself into the driver's side and making herself comfortable, she adjusted her jeans, the position of the steering wheel and the seat. A quick rummage through the glove compartment revealed a white envelope containing a key marked '302' on a green fob and a small roll of bank notes. She took off the elastic band, fanned slowly through the money and took a sharp intake of breath.

"My lucky day!" she smiled excitedly.

She raised her bum out of the chair to retrieve the other wad of cash from her pocket and then tossed it together with the elastic band on the passenger seat. The envelope read 'York, P4' in red ink. Frowning thoughtfully to herself, she threw it onto the passenger seat beside the cash. She took her purse out of her handbag and paused as she gazed at a dog-eared photograph behind a clear plastic window on the outside. It was a faded picture of a pretty young woman, in her early thirties or thereabouts, holding a baby and smiling straight at the camera. Everything seemed to pause for Rachel in that instant.

"I'll find you Mum, I promise I will," she whispered sadly as she stroked the image with her thumb.

With a sigh, Rachel snapped away from the picture as a sense of urgency crept into her thoughts and quickened her movements. She swept up the money, arranged it neatly into her purse, folded the envelope with the key in and slipped it into her purse alongside other scraps of paper. As she pressed gently on the accelerator with her eyes closed, she smiled as she listened to the engine purr and gently caressed the steering wheel with both hands. She took a deep intake of breath and eased the car into gear.

*　*　*　*　*

Meanwhile, back in the hotel room upstairs, the unrecognisable heap beneath the duvet had dragged itself out of bed. After a swift visit to the bathroom to empty his bursting bladder, he realised that his watch, wallet and keys had vanished.

"Bitch!" he spat beneath his breath.

Angrily, he threw back the duvet across the bed and ran his hands under the pillows. Smiling sarcastically to himself, he cursed his own foolery in trusting her; he should have known something would happen.

"Bitch!" he spat again.

He turned to the bedside table and pulled the drawers open violently then sat on the edge of the bed with his head in his hands. With a frustrated sigh, he rubbed his face before he reached for his jacket on the floor beside the bed. From the inside pocket, he retrieved his mobile phone.

"Thank god you never took that!" he whispered angrily, "Bitch!"

He stared at the numbers for a moment, stabbed the buttons with his thumb and paused for a deep breath before he tapped the little green phone. In the next instant, he hit the cancel button, paced around the other side of the room and sat down on the chair. Again he dialled and again he stopped the call before it had connected. He stood for a moment and took a deep breath.

"I've got to," he thought to himself, "just get it over with!"

With a worried sigh, he paced again, raised the phone to his ear and waited for a reply.

8

"Dave? Yeah, I got bad news, Dave. Real bad news," he began with a trembling voice, "I got done over some time last night! Some bitch has taken my wallet and keys! She's cleaned me out, even got my Rolex!"

There was a pause as he listened to the reply from inside the phone. He stood still, pinched the top of his nose lightly with his thumb and forefinger and rubbed gently as he looked out of the window over the balcony.

"Well I could go and check but she's taken the keys. No doubt she would have found the car and that would have gone too!"

He leaned to look out of the window but could not see enough of the car park below to check if his car was still there or not. He stuttered and gesticulated as the other person shouted in his ear.

"No, no, nobody special. Just a whore, you know how it is on these long jobs! Some blonde tart from the bar downstairs; called herself Candy."

Another pause and he nodded. He wiped his brow with his trembling hand and paced up and down again.

"I'll wait. Be quick! If she's found it we're in the shit!"

He rubbed the back of his neck and sighed, lowered the phone from his ear and tossed it onto the bed. Surrendering to his frustration and anger, he sat in an armchair looking out over the balcony. The view of the city was grey and smoky with a smeared golden haze in the early morning autumnal sun. He tapped his fingers furiously on the arm of the chair. The sound of the traffic grew steadily as he fell deeper and deeper into a disturbed trance. He stared blankly into the distance with his fingers drumming louder and louder, faster and faster. When his nerves became too much for him to sit with, he paced up and down. He went into the bathroom and splashed cold water over his face. The minutes dragged on and on as he waited impatiently. The temptation to leave tugged at him, but the consequences warned him against it. He sat, he paced and he waited. Suddenly, there was a firm knock at the door and he jumped up quickly.

"Thank god you're here. What took you so long?" he said as he ushered them in.

"Ricky! What have you done to us?" questioned a large muscular man as he pulled up his collar and adjusted his cufflinks, "All that planning! All that hard work! We were this close to gettin' it done!" he raised his finger and thumb in a symbolic gesture.

He pushed Ricky back as he stepped into the room and was followed by another broad man in a suit and dark glasses. The second man turned and locked the door behind him. The subtle click of the lock sliding into place sounded like a bullet from a gun to Ricky and sent a wave of fear shooting through his limbs. He swallowed hard; beads of sweat gathered on his forehead and the veins in his temples became raised.

"You stupid little sod, Ricky! All because you can't keep it in your fucking trousers! What is it with you? You're worse than our Carl!" he pointed to his associate behind him with his thumb, "Every job we send you on, you get careless! Stupid little shit!"

Ricky felt cold shivers tremble across his skin as his knees weakened. His stomach somersaulted and wrapped itself in knots. Carl smiled a menacing smile from behind Dave.

"Well, not any more Ricky, this one has cost us!" Dave spoke in a threatening tone and slowly approached Ricky.

Carl loomed up from behind Dave and filled Ricky's field of vision.

"It's one too many, Ricky. No more mistakes!" he added.

"Oh Shit! I know I fucked up but…."

Dave raised his finger to his lips and whispered,

"Shush, Ricky. That's enough!"

"We can talk…."

"Shut it!" added Carl.

"But…."

Carl stepped forward and pushed Ricky by the shoulders into the middle of the room. Dave stepped aside with his hands clasped in front of him and stood like an on-looking alter boy. Ricky's world seemed to enter slow motion as the sinister figures intimidated and threatened him. Carl forced the sweating, trembling Ricky into a chair. He lowered his face so their noses almost touched and fixed him in the eye with a freezing stare.

"Now what do we do with you?" he growled slowly.

* * * * *

Rachel flicked on the CD player in the car and gave each track a quick listen. Although the bass was booming and the sound was clear, she did not like anything she heard so she flicked the switch to put the radio on. A couple of channels later and she found something she could nod her head to as she drove down the main road and out onto the motorway. She put her foot down hard and sped off into the fast lane to the sound of electric guitar solos and screaming vocals. The windows and the sunroof slid open at the touch of a button and she flicked back her hair as it blew in the wind. She loved the feeling of driving fast; the wind and the speed made her feel excited and sexy. The car hugged the road like nothing else she had driven and the power in the engine purred beckoningly. She caressed the steering wheel and shuffled herself in against the soft leather seat; the attraction of the throbbing engine was almost sexual, the gentle vibration through the seat was mesmeric and tantalising. She knew she would have to dump the car soon but she tried not to let the thought stop her enjoying her moment. As the speedometer smoothed its way into triple figures, a police car appeared in the rear view mirror with blue lights flashing but no sirens. Rachel slowed down, indicated correctly and joined the central lane. With a fluttering stomach as the car drew closer in her wing mirror, she held her breath as it drove past. She exhaled with a quick whistle and shook her head. When the car was out of sight and the feeling of paranoid guilt and nervousness had subsided, she sped back into the fast lane. She left the motorway at a familiar exit into an industrial town and carried on through the centre to a run down housing estate. Having spent a substantial part of her childhood here, she knew the area and the kind of lives that were being lived in the ramshackle old council houses. If her choice of career had done

one good thing for her, it had elevated her from the deprived neighbourhoods that were all too familiar. A host of childhood memories flooded into her mind and the sight of the unforgettable landmarks reminded her how she stumbled into her line of work.

She recalled giving out kisses to older boys in return for cigarettes in her later years of junior school as she drove passed the old school gates, now railed and padlocked against the unwanted adults since the onset of paedophobia. She remembered how she felt it was unimportant at the time and her peers never frowned at her behaviour. The crushed cans that lined the fence and the broken bottles shattered in the gutters reminded her of the offers of oral sex she made in return for alcohol before she looked old enough to buy it for herself. It was around that time that her social circle began to collapse as the girls took on differing values and attitudes towards their lives. Rachel had begun a downward spiral, she accepted that now but had had no such realisation at the time when it would have been important; when she could have made a difference. As she reminisced, she drove passed a bus shelter where she used to wait on long, cold winter evenings for young drivers to collect her. She remembered how she used to masturbate young men so she could spend time out of her house but not be out on the streets. A slimy hand and a stain on her skirt was a small price to pay for the warmth of a car on long, cold, wet evenings. A dank alleyway caught her eye and like the sickening aftertaste of something unpleasant, the memory of the first time she earned money for penetrative sex regurgitated into her thoughts. She remembered the air stank of urine and stray cats, the man's breath reeked of nicotine and alcohol and the unpleasant warm, moist feeling between her legs emphasised her nausea. Rachel squirmed in her seat as she remembered the cold, harsh, brick wall against her back; how it grazed her spine through her clothes. The more memories her surroundings dredged up, the more she began to realise that she had never had sex without payment in one way or another. She had lost her virginity for money, long after she had lost her dignity for cheap substitutes for happiness.

She shook her head and tried to think of someone that she had made love with for the sake of being in love. She tried so hard to remember; perhaps a teenage lover she had forgotten about; a romantic gesture at the end of a pleasant evening; but the happy memories were not there. If she wanted regrets, unpleasant anecdotes or uncomfortable feelings then she could summon those in abundance, but thoughts of loving or being loved, thoughts of friendship, companionship, being wanted, were absent. She screwed her eyes tight for a moment, in a successful attempt to stop herself weeping. Her stomach turned and she shook her head to disperse the unpleasant feelings and tried to focus on the moment. Slowly and carefully, she scanned the area for a suitable place to leave the car. She crawled down a long straight road lined with run-down buildings with boarded up windows then pulled up in a lay-by outside what was once a popular chip shop. She looked up at the flat above.

"I can't say it's nice to see you again," she thought, suppressing another host of memories.

She gathered up her things and took one last look through the car, rounded the back and opened the boot. Pausing as she scanned, she then leaned over to get a crumpled rag next to a tool kit and empty petrol can. Conscientiously, she wiped all the surfaces in the car with the rag, being careful not to touch anything else. She tossed the rag on the back seat, left the keys in the ignition and pushed the door shut with her foot after she stepped out.

She walked out of sight around to the back of the chip shop. The yard was a small square with two large, metal bins and a pile of plastic crates against the wall. It was exactly as she remembered it. After sealing away a few more unpleasant memories, she pushed her back up to the wall and peered round the corner to the road. She took a deep breath and bit her lower lip in anticipation when she saw two young teenagers in tracksuits walking towards the car. One of them held his hands up to the driver-side window like a pair of binoculars and peered in. The other looked up and down the street and Rachel ducked back behind the wall as he turned in her direction. She heard them talking but could not make out what they were saying. She waited a moment before she turned round to see what was happening. The boys had gone.

"Shit!" she whispered and she turned back to the yard.

She took a plastic crate off the pile, placed it upside-down on the floor and sat on it with her back against the wall and her ankles crossed in front of her. A gathering of ants creeping around the concrete entertained her for a few minutes before she heard the distinctive sound of a car door slamming shut. Peering around the wall saw the two boys sitting in the car with an older boy in the driving seat. With a screech and an audible cheer, they sped off down the street. Rachel smiled, lifted her mobile and phoned for a taxi.

* * * * *

Just before noon, a maid had discovered Ricky's body, strapped with his own belt into a chair with his hands tied behind his back. Badly beaten, his face was almost unrecognisable. There was a single bullet hole in the centre of his forehead and a gaping hole at the base of his skull. Sprayed across the wall and floor behind him were the missing fragments of his head. The forensic officer at the scene confirmed that it was highly probable that the gunshot was the cause of death.

"You don't say!" Detective Inspector Ford sneered then turned to his officers,

"This used to Matthew Richards, 'Ricky' to his so-called pals," he continued, "Stupid bugger upset someone but I doubt anyone will mourn his passing!"

The detective and his team were searching the room. A police officer outside the door was taking a statement from a very distressed maid who cried constantly throughout her interview. Two officers in white paper overalls analysed the walls and floor for clues and took photographs of all the bloodstains and pieces of sheared skull, which had been marked with little plastic numbers.

"There was a girl with him," stated a constable in a matter-of-fact tone as he held aloft a lace bra that he had found under the duvet.

"Assume nothing, Kent, though it looks too small to be his!" Ford joked as he pointed to Ricky with his thumb, "Bag it 'n' tag it and lets find out who she is shall we?"

* * * * *

Rachel's flat was far too big for her needs. She knew that, but as she had grown up in a series of damp, run-down homes, with woodchip wallpaper and draughty doors, she thought she would be as extravagant as she could now she was earning good money. Besides, after what she had been through to establish herself with the clientele she had on her books, she felt she deserved some compensation. She wanted the best she could afford and that allowed her to have more rooms than she knew what to do with. The walls were neutral shades and the woodwork varnished to enhance the natural beauty of the grain. She had a few pieces of expensive furniture that she had found in various antique and second-hand shops that looked rather lonely in the spacious rooms beneath the high Georgian ceilings.

She flicked on the kettle, made herself a coffee and then snuggled into her favourite armchair in the sitting room. With the contents of her handbag spread across the table she took the pieces of scrap paper out of her purse. She sipped her coffee as she read the address on the envelope.

"My guess is you fit a railway locker," she thought to herself as she looked at the key, "and what wonderful goodies will you have for me there?"

She unfolded another scrap of paper and placed it next to the first. It had the telephone number of the local registrars' office on it and the contact details for two adoption agencies. She had scribbled beneath the second of the phone numbers during her personal quest, which had been running for some time now. It was hard work, but she felt like she was getting somewhere and the answers she needed were not too far away. Smiling to herself with a sense of achievement she read through the notes and felt pleased with her progress. Continuing her happy hunt through the contents of her handbag, she took the money from her purse and counted it again. With her fee from the client, the money she stole and the roll of notes in the car, she had in excess of £2,300. Most local retailers would not take fifty-pound notes because they were too easy to forge, so she separated them and put them aside. The remainder would be enough for her to have a decent night out with a meal and drinks. She went over to a drawer in a sideboard and placed the fifty-pound notes in a brown envelope together with a payment slip for her bank.

"Sort that tomorrow, I think," she whispered happily to herself.

She took an apple from a fruit bowl on the sideboard and then slumped back into her chair, pulling her feet up on the cushion. With a sigh she looked at the photograph in her purse as she sipped more coffee. Thoughtfully, she gazed at the woman as she munched on the fresh, crisp Braeburn. She placed her cup on the table and phoned the first of the numbers on the list. Rachel recognised the registrar's voice and reminded him that they had spoken before. The registrar confirmed that he had Rachel's details but needed to confirm a few particulars for security reasons. Rachel responded to the questions and the satisfied registrar offered to meet with her the next day. Rachel agreed and scribbled the time on the piece of paper. She finished her apple and the coffee, gathered up her things from the table and disappeared upstairs.

The shower was warm and refreshing as Rachel washed herself slowly. She stood motionless with her chin up towards the water to let the hot streams flow over her face and down her body. She let the negative thoughts and feelings, stirred up by her journey through her childhood, wash away with the suds. She touched herself lovingly, with care and affection. She always had the most luxurious soaps and shampoos in her bathroom and indulged herself sensually in her shower. The heavy scents filled the room and Rachel soon felt wrapped in comfort. This was her release, her escape, her way of forgetting her life for a while before she had to leave the sanctuary of her bathroom and venture out into the wild world.

She stepped out of the shower and wrapped a towel around her hair. Taking a contraceptive cap and a tube of spermicide cream from her bathroom cabinet, she sat on the edge of the bath. She smeared the cream over the cap and opened her legs slightly to ease insertion. Rubbing her hips and thighs over the towels as she went, she waddled through to her bedroom, where she delicately applied a combination of powders and perfumes to her appreciative body. Then she settled in front of a large mirror to set her hair while it was still slightly damp. She had an array of attachments for her hairdryer and a selection of styling tongs laid out on the floor like precision instruments. She selected her tools carefully and lingered over her pleasurable task of getting her hair exactly how she wanted it to be. When she was almost finished she pulled out a black dress from her cupboard, which she laid neatly across her bed. She tugged at an old oak drawer and battled to get it open. It continuously became stuck on the runner and required several forced attempts until it had opened enough to allow her to reach a pair of black lace knickers and matching hold-up stockings. She slid into the underwear and dropped the dress over her head, carefully avoiding her hair. She turned to the mirror and straightened out the dress. She applied the tongs to her hair for a finishing touch and then switched everything off at the wall socket before she arranged them all in the same order they were in before she had begun.

A car horn pipped outside just as she reached the bottom of her stairs. The taxi was clearly visible in the street outside as Rachel pulled open a curtain slightly, to check that it was calling for her. She picked up her smart black Prada handbag and transferred her purse and keys from her scruffy 'Old Faithful' still on the coffee table. The car pipped again.

"Alright, alright, I'm coming" she murmured.

* * * * *

The Grand Hall of the Masonic Lodge was a beautifully decorated and elegant space. Ornate chandeliers hung from a high ceiling and cast a delicate sheen on all below. Large portraits of past Masons and scenes of landowners hunting with hounds in Olde England looked down on the wealthy and influential clientele as they socialised. The deep red velvet chairs around the tables in the middle of the room complimented the red leather furniture around the periphery. A large, highly polished parquet dance floor stretched in front of the stage where a string quintet entertained the graceful couples as they waltzed enchantingly. Around the floor, tastefully chic tables were dressed and set with silver cutlery, patiently awaiting the attention of those that had come to dine.

A middle-aged man in a navy blue suit and a young woman in an elegant dress sat at one table. Her body language was more than enough to let any curious onlooker know that she did not want to be there with him. His face was glowing red around his nose and cheeks and he slouched back in his chair. His drunken eyes wandered as they tried to focus on the comings and goings of the strangers in the middle distance. She sat with her legs crossed, slightly turned away from him and sipped her wine as she surveyed other diners that had begun to make themselves comfortable around nearby tables. Her attention was elsewhere and the man was busily thinking of ways to get her to turn back to him.

"It's a high rishk business," he boasted as he raised his glass, "shtocks and shares in a vol-hic-tile market!" he continued in a drunken tone.

His female company rolled her eyes, looked up at the beautifully painted ceiling and shook her head slowly. She knew it was her part to listen and humour this arrogant man, after all, he had paid for her company but she begrudged working with such crude, intoxicated creatures. She turned towards him and instantly noticed the flakes of white dandruff resting on the shoulders of his jacket. Her stomach turned. She desperately tried to look interested but could not find it in herself to do anything other than smile politely and sip her wine.

"Do you know hic mush money I made last year?" he asked her as he leaned forward onto the table and rested on his elbow.

His face was close enough for her to be taken aback by the smell of alcohol and tobacco on his breath. She thought about giving him back his £200, but then she thought again. He had probably forgotten about that by now, she thought, especially after so much wine in such a short time. She turned away in disgust and saw someone she knew coming in through the main entrance. A wave of relief came of over her and she sighed pleasurably. She excused herself, almost politely, and skipped off towards her friend.

"Three-an-'alf million!" he slurred to himself before he gulped the last of his wine and slammed his glass on the table next to the empty bottle.

Rachel stood in the archway at the top of the stairs overlooking the room and scanned the guests. Like an elegant hostess, she smiled politely as she looked down on the gathering before her. Suddenly, in amongst the unknown faces she noticed Lisa walking towards her with a broad smile and open arms. Rachel carefully stepped down the few steps leading into the room and met her friend in a hug.

"Save me, save me!" pleaded Lisa humorously exaggerating her voice, "I'm so glad you're here!"

"How's it going?" asked Rachel.

"Same old porkers with fancy drinks and fat wallets slurping and drooling all over themselves!"

"Business good?" Rachel looked out across the room, scanning the men.

"You've got to be joking! There's some serious money in here tonight, but the quality is somewhat lacking. Only saving grace is that these middle-aged farts get so ratted they can't do anything to you at the end of the evening! Shame you have to put up with their slaver all night! You should meet the slobbering idiot I've hooked up with!"

Lisa turned and took Rachel by the hand. They walked over to the bar, slowly and carefully, smiling seductively at the men and looking them up and down. This exclusive club had become a regular meeting place for the girls; the staff knew and accepted them. Business here was easy, especially on a night like this one with middle-aged clients, getting too drunk too quickly. Most of the men were wealthy through working long hours and had become so committed to their businesses that they had neglected their home life and their personal relationships.

Resultantly, they found themselves trapped in loveless marriages, held together only by purse strings and tradition. They liked to pour their hearts out with the girls most of the evening, which was not uncommon, possibly because they never spoke privately to their partners or maybe they found it easier to talk to a stranger. Either way, the girls did not mind, it made their work easier. They would listen on a superficial level, offer no judgement and reply only when it seemed they had to. Sex was not an important part of the transaction for the talkative kind. They often thought they were obliged to perform at some stage in the proceedings because they had paid for the service, although it was usually over quite quickly. The girls had become experts in saying exactly what the men wanted to hear and faking full orgasms within the two-minutes of sexual activity. The pretence was sad, but the money was excellent.

The two girls did however, land an occasional catch that would pay them well and treat them with respect. If they were really lucky, they may even enjoy the sex. The man Lisa had left slurring into his own drunken ego had lit a fat cigar and raised his hand in an attempt to regain her attention. He was the opposite of everything she hoped for in a client and had begun to regret replying to his on-line booking without seeing him first. Lisa pretended not to notice him. She giggled to Rachel and lowered her gaze. When they reached the bar they ordered their drinks and turned again to look out across the room.

"Don't you just hate these money spinners' balls?" asked Lisa, thoughtfully after a short pause to scan the surroundings.

"Not really," replied Rachel, "this is my bread and butter! These slobbering old fools are my pension fund!" she grinned.

"I'll get those!" said a smart gentleman in a tailored suit as he walked towards the girls.

"Drinks for these two gorgeous ladies all night on my tab, Jason," he added.

"Yes Sir, Mr Johnson, as you wish," the waiter nodded his head obediently and passed the drinks to the women.

"Forgive me," he began, holding out his hand by way of introduction, "I'm Peter Johnson."

"I know you!" started Lisa as she shook his hand, "You're the guy that won the lottery and started that business scheme thing for drug addicts right?"

"That would be me, yes," he nodded modestly.

"Well fancy meeting you here!" Rachel added as she shook his hand also.

"Please, would you care to join me for the evening?"

The two women looked at each other and nodded in unison.

"Of course," smiled Rachel.

"Love to," smiled Lisa.

They went over to a large round table near the back wall in the dimmed light and made themselves comfortable. The conversation began around the décor, the general ambience of the hall and then turned to people watching. They amused each other and boosted their individual egos as they judged the characters that dined and danced. Peter liked to talk about his achievements. He was obviously proud of his foundation scheme for alcoholics and drug addicts and he mentioned large sums of money whenever he could. Although Rachel considered the deliberate show of wealth as quite vulgar and detected some kind of unnerving undertone, she smiled politely and kept in with the conversations. Lisa was impressed by him, Rachel could see that; anyone in the room could have seen that had they looked. She fixed her eyes on his all evening and constantly smiled at him, seemingly transfixed. They talked, laughed and drank wine for almost three hours before they ordered their meals. The food was fabulous, expensive and paid for by Peter. After three courses and coffee they continued talking and sat closer and closer to each other. Peter sat upright and puffed out his chest as he tried hard to hold in his middle-aged spread. His posture boasted his pride while flanked by two beautiful young women. He reached out and touched Lisa's knee whenever he laughed or added a quirky comment to her anecdotes and she relished the attention. When Peter sat back and tried to put his arm around Rachel's shoulders she shook her head and pushed his hand away gently.

"You have to pay for me," she whispered quietly.

After a short silence, Lisa added,

"Me too."

Peter frowned and looked at both the women with a down-turned mouth. His face looked saddened and disappointed. He shook his head as he spoke.

"Well…" he began slowly, "I'm sure you are worth every penny!" he said as he raised his face with a wide grin, "Excuse me while I find us a room."

Peter left the two ladies to chat and he disappeared through the archway.

"He's not bad for his age, is he?" started Lisa.

"Not bad at all – and he's loaded!" added Rachel.

"It wasn't a jackpot win was it? Was he one of those that had to share it with a few others?" Lisa quizzed with a lowered voice.

"Yeah, yeah, but still – he's loaded!" giggled Rachel quietly.

They talked about his square jaw, firm figure and swapped judgements on his wrinkles and greying hair. They were both in agreement that in his case, he had aged distinctively and they considered him to be a very handsome man, albeit his wealth had added to his handsomeness. A few minutes later he reappeared at the table and shook a room key in front of the women like a master's bell to summon his servants.

"Party time!" he smiled.

The three left the table and staggered over to the exit. Peter walked behind and watched the swaying motion of their hips. The two women had their arms around each other for mutual support although they both knew that they pretending to be more intoxicated than they actually were. It was not a good idea to drink too much while they were working, especially here where the establishment expected a better-behaved clientele. They waited outside the lift for the doors to open. Peter stood in the middle with an arm around each waist. The two women returned the embrace. A young man almost fell out of the lift when the doors slid back and bumped into the trio.

"Give 'em one from me mate!" he said in a low tone as he staggered down the corridor.

The three entered the lift and Lisa turned to Peter. She pinned him up against the wall and kissed him passionately. He could feel her warmth and the feint beating of her heart against his chest. Peter's hand slid down her back and caressed her firm buttocks. Rachel nibbled and licked his ear while she stroked his chest gently with her long, painted nails. Peter shuddered uncontrollably for a moment and turned to Rachel. The two women took turns kissing and stroking him until they reached their floor and they strolled out into the corridor.

"Room 241," he smiled, "how very apt!"

No sooner were they through the door than Lisa and Rachel detached themselves from him and suddenly seemed to lose all signs of passion. They stood at the foot of the bed. Peter stood just inside the door, not knowing what to expect. He reached out to the light switch and the two bedside lamps filtered a gentle glow across the subtle tones of the duvet.

"£500," said Lisa, very matter of fact, "each."

"That gets you all night," added Rachel.

"And we do anything you like," whispered Lisa provocatively.

"Anything!" Rachel turned to Lisa and smiled, and then they wrapped their arms around each other.

They acted out a well-rehearsed, deeply passionate kiss so that Peter noticed their tongues touching before their mouths met with open lips.

"That really is not a problem!" said Peter shakily with a hint of nervous excitement.

He reached inside his pocket and pulled out his wallet. Without counting he removed a wad of notes and dropped them onto the bed before he quickly removed his jacket and tie and then began pulling at the buttons of his shirt. Lisa and Rachel undressed each other, slowly, deliberately and with great affection for each other. They took their time to make sure that Peter was aroused to the point of impatience by the time they were both down to their lingerie. Peter stood by the door, naked but for his socks, with an erection pointing out almost humorously. He stroked his penis as he looked at the two outstandingly beautiful women that he had standing in all their

23

lace-embraced glory before him. His excitements rushed inside him like hot waves of want.

"You got to do the right thing," whispered Lisa.

"Got to keep us safe!" added Rachel.

Rachel leaned forward deliberately so that Peter saw as much of her tempting body as possible as she scooped up the money quickly and smoothly. She reached into her handbag, discreetly dropped in the cash and pulled out her purse. Lisa kneeled on the bed with her legs apart and began to remove her bra. Rachel opened her purse and placed a packet of condoms on the bedside table.

"In your own time Peter, put it on," she whispered.

She put her purse on the bedside table, slid back onto the bed and carefully placed her face between Lisa's knees. She kissed her way up Lisa's tender thigh to her lace knickers and gripped the material between her teeth. Lisa gasped and then bit her own finger gently as she looked straight into Peter's eyes. Peter reached over to get a condom; his hands shook with excitement as he stretched out. He momentarily glimpsed down at the purse and caught sight of the photo. With a paranoid hint of recognition, he moved the purse further into the gentle light and looked carefully at the picture. He felt his stomach drop and he came over cold. The hairs on the back of his neck stood on end, as if an icy chill had swept over him. Rachel held Lisa's knickers aside with one hand and gently, tenderly, licked her clitoris. Lisa had leaned forward with her eyes closed and caressed her own breasts with one free hand. The two girls moaned softly and writhed slowly on the bed. Peter, now oblivious to the erotic happenings right next to him, picked up the purse to get a better look. A tremor ran up his spine and he shuddered. He dropped the purse as if it had burned his fingers and stared at the picture staring back at him in the lamplight.

"I can't do this!" he said with his voice shaking as he hopped around trying to put his trousers on.

"Ooh, I bet you, umm, can!" groaned Lisa, still with her eyes closed.

"I got to go!" said Peter as he picked up his shirt and slipped into his shoes.

He scooped his jacket off the floor as he stormed out of the room. He slammed the door behind him with a loud bang. Rachel jolted on the bed, which caused a gentle bite where there ought to have been a kiss and Lisa squeaked with delight. The involuntary expression of excitement spurred Rachel on to play with more passion and she never stopped what she was doing to see what had startled her.

"Hmm, what do you know babe?" Lisa's voice trembled as she spoke; "We were too hot for him!" whispered Lisa as she lowered her head between Rachel's thighs.

Chapter 2

Bedraggled and cold, a young man shuffled down into his makeshift bed as the distant, early morning birdsong woke him from his broken sleep. He had been curled up in his cardboard home, lodged against the cold stone of an alcove set high into a disused railway tunnel all night. The nights were unbelievably long and grim when they were void of sleep. Comfort was a distant memory. He suffered silently as he waited for his limbs to thaw enough for him to move them. He listened to the distant songbirds singing in an attempt to take his mind off the waves of hurt in his limbs. Eventually, he winced in pain as he straightened his legs and stretched out his arms. He arched his back against the harsh stone and pulled his overcoat tight around him to ward off the early morning chill. His clothes were damp and icy cold to the touch. He rummaged through his pockets as gently as he could with his stiffened fingers and pulled out a crumpled packet of cigarettes. He shook his head, annoyed that he had slept on them and possibly ruined his only smokes. After delicately ironing out as many creases as he could from the white paper, he carefully snapped off the filter, placed the cigarette between his lips and then returned his shaking hands to his pockets to find a light. He struck a single match on the wall next to him and cupped his hands around the flame. He lingered momentarily to make the most of the short-lived warmth, which felt like a raging fire against his frozen hands.

He inhaled deeply and held the smoke in his lungs for a long moment before he coughed and spluttered the blue-grey cloud out. The jerking movements of his involuntary action caused more aches and pains to surface as they too woke from their slumber. He inhaled deeply again and lay down on the cardboard beneath him. Every movement was careful and slow. His head spun from the rush of nicotine bringing about a feeling of comfortable, welcoming dizziness. He watched shadows against the stone wall tinge in orange as he inhaled and the end burned brighter. He smoked slowly until the cigarette was so small he could no longer hold on to it without burning his fingers. When the cigarette had gone, he wiped his face with his hands and, hesitantly, jumped down from the alcove.

He dropped like lead onto the harsh gravel with a grunt before he pulled his coat tight and tied the belt around his waist. He pulled up his woollen socks beneath his jeans and tightened his bootlaces, then walked over to the archway of light at the end of the tunnel to emerge into the dawn, cowering from the brightness of the autumnal haze. With his arms stretched wide and a big yawn, he stood by the tracks. The blackbirds and starlings were in full flow, singing out their stories from the rows of dense Hawthorn and Elder down each side of the disused track. He hugged himself with a shudder and then carried on towards the old station where he hopped up onto the platform and across the car park. An old abandoned Renault sat at an awkward angle beneath a street light, inviting him over. He pulled open the door and leaned in. In the glove compartment he found a manual for a portable game console, which he threw on the back seat. He opened the ashtrays, removed several cigarette stubs and put them in his pocket. With his head bowed against the chill, he left the car park and walked along the road. It was not long before he was tapping on a dirty wooden door in a row of terraced houses. He then stepped back to look at the stained curtains, pulled shut across the grubby windows. It was hard to tell if they were dirty yellow or faded brown. There was no answer so he knocked again and shouted up to the bedroom window,

"Mickey? Mickey!"

After a few short moments, there was a muffled sound of thudding as someone came running down the stairs in the hall behind the door. After a short wait, the door opened with a click and a young man in his underwear and T-shirt invited him in.

"Bloody hell, Jack! Do you know what time it is? You wake my neighbours and they'll be moaning at me again. I can do without the grief, mate!" said Mickey, leading him into the living room.

"Got to help me, Mickey! I'm fuckin' freezin'!" Jack's voice shook as he spoke.

Jack fell back onto the sofa and Mickey tried to light the fire. He twisted the knob on the side and the spark plug thudded but the flames never came.

"This thing does my head in!" whispered Mickey, "Got a light, Jack?"

Jack had slumped back on the sofa with his arm across his eyes and although he was not yet sleeping, Mickey thought he would let him rest undisturbed for a while. He shrugged, went through to the kitchen and quickly returned with a lighter. The fire lit within seconds. He returned to the kitchen and put the kettle on. A few minutes later he came into the room with two mugs of coffee and a packet of chocolate bourbons. He put one of the coffees on the floor next to the sofa where Jack was breathing deeply. Making himself comfortable in his favourite spot, he reached down under his armchair and pulled out a stout wooden box with a decorative Celtic knot design around the edges. He took out a small, plastic bag of brown powder and a bent desert spoon, blackened from numerous burnings. He held the bag up to the light filtering through the dirty curtains and smiled as he gave the bag a gentle shake. He slid two hypodermic syringes out of a plastic wallet marked 'Haven Health Services' and took a short, well-used candle from a small compartment in the box. He closed the box and used the lid as a worktop. Like a surgeon preparing his medical instruments for a delicate operation, he arranged his paraphernalia carefully, and after a few minor tinkerings with the positions of his raw materials, proceeded to create Jack and himself a fix each.

"Wakey, wakey sleeping beauty!" he shouted at Jack as he kicked his foot, which hung over the edge of the sofa.

Jack came round slowly with several grunts and groans and took a moment to gather his far-flung thoughts together. Mickey was tightening a plastic tube around his upper arm and holding the loose end in his teeth. He carefully positioned the needle against his embossed vein and pushed. Jack crept over slowly, took the second syringe from the box top and followed a similar ritual. Within a few delicate though energised minutes, both men lay motionless in the room, infinitely comfortable, staring lovingly into their dreams with their mouths slightly open.

Jack had no idea what time it was when he finally came round but he was grateful to recognise the cessation of his withdrawal symptoms. He was aware that his symptoms were little more than irritating as he was still in the early stages of his addiction. He also knew that some time soon, if he did not cease his habit, the severity of hanging out would soon become unbearable. The fire had been burning on full and the room was warm enough to encourage further sleep. The thick heat emphasised the usually subtle, unidentified stale smell that wafted indiscriminately through Mickey's unkempt house. Jack had not felt so comfortable for a long time. He often came to Mickey's in the mornings if he had slept in the tunnel, but up until last night, he had been decking down in a service alley behind a café and a pub. Sleeping was harder but the bins had more to offer.

Mickey was sprawled back in his chair, drooling from the corner of his mouth. Jack leaned over and waved his hand in front of his eyes. When he was sure he was unresponsive he staggered into the kitchen and acquired a small piece of tin foil from a drawer. He came back and checked his responses again. Satisfied that Mickey was still out for the count, Jack helped himself to a scraping of the brown powder from the bag and folded it up in the foil. He slipped it into his sock and went through to the kitchen, taking the mugs with him. By the time he had made two more drinks and gathered some crisps and cakes from the cupboards, Mickey had started to come round. There was a knock at the door.

"Shit!" whispered Jack and he looked around the room in a panic, not knowing what to do with the steaming mugs he had in his hands.

Mickey used his foot to slide the box, still topped with the tools of his trade, under his chair and out of sight.

"OK, just a minute" he called.

He got himself to his feet, rubbed his eyes and inhaled deeply. Jack sat back on the couch, and sipped at his drink nervously. He noticed his syringe on a cushion and quickly swiped it out of sight into his pocket.

"Come in mate," muffled the sound of Mickey's voice from the hallway.

"Alright, Jack? How you doin'?" asked the visitor.

"Not bad, Jonny. You?"

The limited pleasantries tinged with a hint of aggression and distrust were almost enough to allow Jack to relax again. Jack and Jonny had met several times under similar circumstances but neither one would call the other a friend. They had a mutual acceptance that they were necessary partners, but the relationship was purely business. Jonny was a large man, always smartly dressed and had his head shaved. He was a natural intimidator and always spoke down to people with an aggressive overtone. He had a large brown leather bag that he lifted off his shoulder as he sat down next to Jack, who shuffled uncomfortably in his seat.

"Fuckin' hot in here, boys!" he shook his head, "...and it stinks! What died in here?"

He looked sideways at Mickey and sneered.

"Got a deal for ya," he continued slowly, "take this over to Kit's for me. She's waiting for it but I reckon I'm being watched so I have to stay clean. Know what I mean?" he took a large brown package out of his bag, "I took a big risk coming here with this. Treat it with the respect it deserves!"

Jack lit an incense stick from a vase on the hearth and placed it in a holder on the mantle piece.

"OK," answered Mickey nervously, "are you paying the fares?"

"As always Mickey," he smiled as he handed Mickey a £20 note, "plus your usual 10% to the house when the goods are delivered."

Mickey took the money and the package with a smile.

"Very nice, Jonny. What we got here? Couple o' K?" asked Mickey with a wide smile.

"Yeah. You know the score!" he spoke slowly with a voice that Jack found threatening.

Jack shuffled in his seat again and took another sip of his drink as Jonny got up. He raised himself to his full height and towered over Mickey.

"Fuck this up… and I'll fuck you up! Get it?" he said flatly.

"OK" shook Mickey.

Jonny patted Mickey hard on the shoulder with two dull thuds and made his way to the front door unaccompanied. Mickey stood slightly trembling in the centre of his room as he anticipated the sound of the door signalling that Jonny had left the building. Jack just stared up from his seat, eyes wide at the temptation of all that gear in his best mate's hand. They heard the door slam shut on the other side of the wall. Mickey rubbed his shoulder.

"We taking your 10% now then?" Jack asked quickly with an excited tone as he rubbed his hands together in glee.

"Never!" snapped Mickey, "Got to get it to Kit first then she'll cut me in. You know what she's like! If all the gear ain't there when she gets it, I'll get it in the neck with that bloody blade of hers!"

"She still carrying that thing? I thought she gave it up when her kid got taken off her? Didn't they say she could go down for that?" quizzed Jack as he tried his best to recollect a lost conversation from a stoned memory.

"As if she gives a shit! She's mental, that one!"

Mickey walked over to the window and pulled the curtain back a little. He saw Jonny driving off down the street. His relief was short lived when he noticed a telephone repairman across the road, standing at the top of a ladder against a telegraph pole and adjusting the workings. He appeared to look at Mickey and then reach for something in his tool belt. He attached a telephone to a wire in the service box and began to speak. Mickey watched his mouth moving in silence. He looked further down the street towards a van with British Telecom logos on the side and noticed another man sitting in the front seat reading a newspaper. He too seemed to look up at Mickey so he dropped the curtain quickly and took a step back.

"Shit!" he whispered, "they're watching us!"

"What?" Jack jumped up from his chair and went over to the window.

"Don't touch that!" Mickey said as he grabbed Jack's hand before he reached the curtain, "Bastards are out there watching us!" he whispered, "They always pretend to be workmen or something, so you don't know you're being watched! Jonny brought them here I bet. Here, take this out back will you, Jack? Bomb down to Kit's for me and you can have half my cut," he pleaded.

"What? Then they'll get me with it won't they, you freakin' idiot!" Jack shook his head.

"No they won't. Go out back and skip over the wall into next door's. Follow the alley down and you'll come out on Chester Street, down the road from the shops," Mickey gesticulated as he spoke to point out the directions.

Mickey told Jack the directions to the bus stop and gave him some loose change. Jack scribbled Kit's address on the palm of his hand and instinctively put Mickey's pen into his own pocket.

"OK. But make my cut bigger. This is your risk I'm taking here, Mickey," Jack looked him in the eye and the pair stood in silence for an uncomfortably long, thoughtful moment.

"No mate, can't do that," Mickey said, suddenly breaking the stalemate, "but I got some really good weed. You can have a couple of O's when you get back."

"It better be worth it!" added Jack after another short, thoughtful moment.

Jack took the package and bundled it under his coat. When he was confident he had it gripped under his arm and it was not too obvious, he walked through the kitchen to the back door. He spied an unopened packet of cigarettes on the worktop and palmed them into his pocket as he passed, before Mickey had entered the room behind him. Mickey unlocked the back door, slid back the two bolts and removed the chain, then looked around outside.

"That way," he pointed.

Jack stepped out into the overgrown garden and vaulted the wall with one hand to support him. He immediately regretted his gymnastics, as his limbs were not as fully functional as he imagined. He skipped unnoticed across the neighbour's lawn and over the opposite wall with a less sprightly jump. He slipped through an open gate and into the litter-strewn alleyway. As he neared the end of the alley he saw several young girls in school uniforms walking down the street beyond. Some were alone; others were in pairs and small groups.

"Shit! Just in time for the bloody school kids!" he thought, feeling slightly paranoid and self-conscious about his appearance.

He paused to light a cigarette and then walked out onto the street. He stepped straight into the path of a small group of schoolgirls accompanied by three older boys in tracksuits and baseball caps.

"Watch it bag-head!" scowled the first boy.

"Get the fuck out the way, junkie scum!" added another.

"Kick his head in, Kev!" laughed one of the girls.

The other girls joined in and the chant became louder and louder.

"Kick his head in! Kick his head in!"

One of the boys pushed his way passed the girls and squared up to Jack. He pushed his shoulder.

"Maybe I will, bag-head! Wha'd'ya think o' that?" he scowled.

"I'm just walking. I'm going…" Jack stuttered as he looked the boy in the eye.

"No you're not!" smiled the boy and he swung for Jack.

The impact of the punch was not hard and Jack scarcely moved at all. He took a step back and pleaded not to get into a fight. He raised his hands in front of him. The boy stepped forward and swung again but missed. His two friends had circled around Jack. The girls were shouting and the boys were swearing, hurling abuse. A small crowd of schoolgirls, noticing the increasing hostility, had gathered to watch from across the road. Jack tried to walk backwards quickly and get away but the boys would not stop the intimidation. Jack absorbed the impact of another fist that landed on his cheek and gave up trying to escape when he saw they had him surrounded. He threw a punch forward at the lead boy. It connected to his chin and threw him backward onto the floor. He landed at the feet of the girls who instantly became quiet. There was a short scream from across the road followed by exaggerated fits of laughter.

"Get up, Kev! Get him!" snarled one of the girls.

"I don't want any trouble!" Jack pleaded again.

"Too fuckin' late mate!" replied one of the boys.

Jack felt a sharp pain in his ribs and realised instantly he had stabbed him. The boy had a small screwdriver in his hand and swung for Jack again. He stepped sideways to avoid the blow but the other boy had swung a punch to Jack's face and the impact increased as Jack stepped straight into it. He hit the floor and covered his face with his hands. The package came away from his grip and fell out of his coat into the gutter as Jack rolled onto the cold, hard pavement. Vicious feet came at Jack from the front and behind, hitting him all over his upper body and head. Now and again the jab of a heel came down on his torso. In an act of self-preservation, he tucked himself into a ball and wrapped his arms around his head. He shouted for them to stop but they kept on kicking. The sound of the kicks and the screams of the girls grew in his ears. He couldn't tell if they were screaming with delight or with horror.

Suddenly, he whipped out his arms and grabbed a leg as it made contact with his stomach, wrapped his body around the shin like a bear trap and instantly rolled forward, pushing his whole weight onto the leg. Flipped off balance, the boy fell in a pendulum motion like a mightily swung sledgehammer. He fell inescapably and swift like a dead weight with nothing to stop him or break his fall. A mighty crack ordered instant silence from the whole street as the boy's head hit the floor. Jack got up slowly and looked down at the boy who lay motionless on the pavement in a Jesus Christ pose with a steadily growing puddle of blood beneath his head.

The whole world seemed to stop for breath. All onlookers were still and quiet. Most of the girls had their mouths covered with their hands while others had turned to hug their friends. Slowly, the noise around Jack grew steadily louder. The girls were staring at the boy with open mouths and crying eyes. The other two boys were distant figures running off down the street. Jack looked round for the package but it had vanished. He looked at the three girls closest to him and they stared back at him with fear in their eyes. Without thinking, he reached out quick and grabbed the nearest girl by her lapels.

"Who took the stuff?" he demanded, "Who?"

The terrified girl began crying and her words were difficult to hear.

"WHO?" shouted Jack as he shook her back and forth.

There was no audible reply that Jack could understand so, annoyed and frustrated, he pushed the girl back with force. She stumbled and landed in a sitting position on the pavement, sobbing loudly as she stared at the boy on the floor. Jack grabbed another girl by her school tie and pulled her towards him. Her head rocked violently on her shoulders as she stepped forward awkwardly. The girl screamed a name and address, and then Jack let go. He stood for a moment and wobbled on his feet as a dizzy spell ran through his senses. He looked down at his ribs and saw he was bleeding quite badly. It was only when he saw the blood soaking through his clothes that he felt the true immensity of the pain and the reality of the situation settled into his thoughts. Rubbing the area with his hand only increased the throbbing sharpness he felt and he winced as he leaned forward to vomit. Blood and bile splashed onto the pavement and splattered onto the girls' shoes. He turned his gaze to the boy on the floor. The blood puddle was still growing steadily wider and making its way towards the gutter in a tiny red rivulet that followed a crack in the pavement. One of the girls had started shouting into her mobile phone as the other two screamed over her shoulders. Jack snapped out of his painful trance and realised what was happening. He staggered down the alley in an attempted run and headed back to Mickey's place as his senses began to fade and his world began to spin.

* * * * *

In the boardroom on the top floor of his office building Peter sat behind his highly polished desk. From his seat, he could see out over the city with its towering offices and great walls of glass, glimmering in the hazy sun. He stared into the distance as he swung left and right in his swivel chair, rubbing his chin with the end of a remote control unit, pondering. Occasionally, his gaze dropped to a large envelope on the desk in front of him. He sat in undisturbed silence until there was a gentle knock at the door.

"Come in," he stated flatly, as he rose to his feet.

A smartly dressed young woman stepped inside the room and held the door open for two tall men in suits that walked slowly behind her. When the men were in the room, she turned and left. Peter stood to greet the men with a firm handshake and offered them a seat. The first man sat down opposite Peter, pulled his shirt collar up and adjusted his sleeves by tugging at his cufflinks. The second man stood behind him with his arms folded.

"You both know why you're here?" Peter questioned rhetorically, almost stating a fact.

The two men never responded at all. They were silent and motionless, like giant stone gargoyles.

"I saw a ghost last night, gentlemen, and that concerns me!" Peter spoke very matter-of-fact as he pushed the envelope across the table to the seated man.

"Now I don't know if I'm being haunted or if it's just a coincidence, but I need that ghost followed. I want to know which crypt it crawled out of and why it's floating around. If it comes to it," he paused, "I may require a little exorcism."

The seated man tilted his head over to one side and narrowed his eyes. Peter clicked the remote control and a large screen flicked into life at the end of the room. There was an image of Rachel stepping out of a taxi, followed by several more sequential scenes taken as she walked from the taxi to the front door of her flat.

"Her address is in the envelope with copies of these photos. Stay on her. Day and night - I want to know who she is, what she does, where she goes, everything!" he demanded.

The seated man stood up in silence. He pulled his collar and adjusted his sleeves again, then nodded to Peter. The man standing behind him waited and then followed him out of the door. Peter flicked back through the images and rubbed his chin with the remote control. He rocked back and forth on his heels as he stood flicking through the images in silence. He stared for a few minutes and then threw the remote control violently against the wall. It smashed with a loud crack and the broken fragments slid along the table and scattered across the floor.

The two men sat in a smart black Jaguar outside the building across the street. The man in the passenger seat tore the envelope neatly to get to the contents.

"What do you think, Carl?" he asked as he slid the papers out of the envelope.

"Someone got him scared this time, Dave. I don't know who she is but she scares him!" he shook his head as he turned the key in the ignition.

"Yeah... just what I thought," his accomplice nodded as he flicked through the photos. He selected one with the best view of her face to put on top of the others.

"She's a saucy one, ain't she eh?" he showed the photo to the driver, "I wouldn't say no!"

"You wouldn't say no to anyone! That's why you're always down the clinic you filthy twat!" he joked.

Dave put the photographs on the dashboard and tilted the envelope to get to the papers at the bottom. A slip of white notepaper with an address on it fell onto his lap, closely followed by six wads of cash held together with bankers' seals.

"£6,000? Just to keep tabs? He's serious about this one!" Dave puzzled as he fanned the cash.

The car pulled away from the kerb and headed in the direction of the address on the paper, which led them to a wide street overlooking a large park with an ornamental pond. The old Georgian terraced houses had stairs leading up to the front doors and tall rectangular windows on all three storeys. Some had skylights and satellite dishes that looked out of place among the historical buildings. Many on the terrace were luxury flats for the lucrative 'young professional' markets as the houses alone were out of range for the local salaries.

"Nice place," nodded Dave "What do you think, Carl?"

"All right I suppose," he replied shrugging his shoulders, "If you've got enough dough!"

They pulled up outside the park in a vacant parking bay. Dave looked out of his window towards the terrace, scanning for Rachel's flat.

"That one, there," he said as he tapped the car window, "the greeny-blue one."

He slid down in his seat and pulled out a newspaper. Carl took the photographs off the dashboard. He looked at each one in turn, compared the image of the doorway to the real one across the road and nodded.

"What we doing about the locker?" quizzed Carl as he returned the pictures to the dashboard.

"I got Sammy looking after it. He's keeping his eyes peeled for us. Don't worry about it, Carl."

"Sammy? Is he reliable enough? He's let us down before you know. If we lose that..." started Carl.

"Don't worry about it. It's safe."

Dave held up his hand up as if to stop Carl's words in mid-air. Momentarily startled, he then dropped his attention to his paper. Carl hated when Dave cut him off but he never challenged him on it. He had come to learn that Dave usually had all the right answers and he did not have to think too long or too hard about things. It was a beneficial relationship for Carl; Dave did the brainwork and Carl did as he was told.

He looked out into the street and tapped his fingers on the steering wheel. In his boredom, Carl let his eyes and mind wander as he searched for something to keep him occupied. Across the park he admired a young woman in a short skirt walking her dog. He followed her legs as they passed by his window, flickering in and out of view through the metal railings. As she vanished out of his line of sight, he turned his attention to his wing mirror, which after a slight adjustment allowed him to watch her walk for a while longer. He gazed out the front of the car and saw a couple of young lads kick a football to each other as they drank cheap lager from the cans. A beautiful woman across the street caught his eye. She had knee-high boots and a short, pale skirt with a wider hem that flittered in the breeze, matching her long blonde hair that flowed out behind her as she walked. Her coat was a thick furry jacket and she had a bag strapped over her shoulder.

"That's her!" Carl snapped as he turned the key in the ignition.

Dave sat up quickly, folded the paper and dropped it into the foot well. He raised his arm across the steering wheel in a 'wait-for-it' gesture as he watched the girl walking away from them. When he thought Rachel had walked a reasonable distance away he removed his arm and Carl pulled out into a U-turn. Carl misjudged the turn and mounted the kerb slightly on the opposite side of the road. The lads with the football shouted humorous abuse at his obviously poor effort, and Carl replied with his middle finger raised in an abusive salute. When he had the car lined up in the correct lane, they followed Rachel to the end of the street at a very slow pace.

"This is too suspicious!" Dave said as he shook his head, "Let me out and I'll walk. You wait back at the flat until I call you."

Carl pulled over and Dave jumped out.

Carl looked thoughtfully at the roadside opposite and glimpsed the lads in his rear view mirror.

"Oh sod it!" he whispered to himself as he reversed down the length of the road and parked up by the kerb.

Dave followed Rachel on foot. It was a brisk walk into the Town Centre and Dave kept a reasonable distance behind. Rachel walked quite quickly, clicking along in her high-heels, skipping up kerbs and dashing out across roads whenever a convenient lull appeared in the traffic. Dave kept up the trail at a discreet distance and he soon found himself slightly out of breath in a part of town he had seldom passed through before. Feeling a little lost, he looked around quickly but a few skyline-landmarks later gave him a vague idea of where he was. More at ease, he followed her in the busy shopping precinct where he could become inconspicuous among the crowds of oblivious shoppers. He followed her through a large chemist's shop where she bought what Dave considered to be a large supply of condoms and a tube of cream of some sort. She picked up a prescription in a small paper bag and then wandered slowly through the store to the exit.

They emerged onto a large pedestrianised area, on the far side of the precinct, with seating and raised ornamental flowerbeds. When she meandered happily into the lingerie section of a large department store, Dave hovered on the periphery like an embarrassed schoolboy. He watched as she picked out a lace negligée and two pairs of knickers. He walked away casually but made sure he could still see Rachel in one of the many mirrored columns throughout the store. She stopped to admire various handbags and shoes as she ambled her way towards the checkout. She mooched through the precinct, in and out of shops as she went, for most of the afternoon. She stopped for coffee in Nobles, a café with chairs and tables outside. Dave took the opportunity to rest and have a coffee himself. He had not long made himself comfortable when he saw her finish her drink and get up quickly. He gulped the hot remainder of his coffee, which slightly burned the roof of his mouth, and followed after her before she disappeared from sight. She left the crowded precinct and started down a long straight road towards Town Hall Square. She crossed the busy road at one of the many pedestrian crossings but Dave missed the lights and had to wait. He watched her disappear into the Registry Office as he frantically pressed the little button, as if pushing several times would speed up the process. He looked up and down the row of traffic but no crossable gap appeared.

He walked briskly through the throng of shoppers on the crossing to the sound of the green man beeping as he made a beeline for Town Hall Square. The historic Town Hall, Registry Office and the Municipal Offices all stood together around an ornate courtyard with a green, copper statue of Queen Victoria in the centre. He went over to a decorative bench where he could watch and wait for her. He passed the time studying the stone carvings and statuettes on the walls of the old buildings surrounding the Square. The sandstone blocks with grand carvings would have been impressive once upon a time. Now those once influential people were featureless due to a century and a half of weather and had become almost unrecognisable.

The sandstone had darkened with age and exhausts' fumes and the pigeons too had left their mark. It was almost an hour before she emerged again. She paused at the top of the steps just outside the doorway to slip some papers into her bag. She came across the Square and headed toward Dave, sat on the bench. She looked straight at him with a lingering gaze and a subtle hint of a smile. He instinctively smiled in reply as she walked straight passed him and towards the bus station. She jumped onto a number forty-two just as it pulled away from the stop.

"Shit!" he whispered as he neared the station.

He watched the bus as it sailed passed him, slowly at first but accelerating all the while. He could see her walking down the aisle towards the back of the bus. He pulled his mobile phone from his inside pocket and called Carl.

"I'm at the Bus Station, mate. She got the forty-two. Don't know where it goes. Keep 'em peeled. I'll be there in thirty."

* * * * *

Mickey paced up and down the length of his front room with beads of sweat building on his forehead. He ran his fingers through his hair and repeated "Shit!" in a shivering voice over and over again. Jack was leaning forward as he sat on the couch, holding his ribs where blood was slowly flowing from his wound,

"I'm getting cold Mickey!" he trembled, "Real cold...."

He sobbed as he held out his other hand and looked closely at his fading fingers. Mickey continued to pace, seemingly unmoved by Jacks predicament but obviously more concerned with the fact that it was happening in his home.

"What the fuck! Jack?" he stuttered.

Jack slid off the couch and keeled over like a felled tree into the centre of the carpet. He rolled onto his back and his hand hit the hearth with a crack.

"Shit!" spat Mickey, "What the fuck...?"

He paced again and started to sob but made no attempt to help Jack at all. He looked down at his face, then closed his eyes as he turned deathly pale. Jack's clothes had become dark and wet around his wound. Traces of blood highlighted as they caught little shafts of daylight that filtered in through the curtains.

"Shit!" he cried openly with tears streaming down his face.

He instinctively slid the wooden box out from beneath his chair and lifted the lid, then paused as a cloak of guilt wrapped around him like a shroud and he pushed the box back into its hiding place. He jumped up and rubbed his face. His skin was cold and clammy and his insides trembled and shivered uncontrollably. He thought about calling for an ambulance but worried about the police. The thought of all the drugs that he had around the house, weighed, measured and wrapped ready for selling would not allow him to get caught.

"Shit, shit, shit, shit!" he whimpered as he wrestled with the choices before him.

He slid his hands down one side of the couch and rummaged behind the cushions; again on the other side and then in his armchair. Eventually, he pulled out his mobile phone and thumbed through his numbers. Shaking with fear to such an extent, he could not hit the buttons accurately. After several attempts to scroll through his phonebook, he managed to find the number he was looking for and make the call.

"Jonny? Come quick! Jack's dead!" he spoke quickly through his tears.

He folded the phone shut, dropped it onto the chair and fell to his knees beside Jack. He rocked forward and back with his head in his hands as his tears rolled down his face and neck.

"You bastard, Jack!" he whispered as he punched down on his chest.

"You fucking bastard!" he whispered louder.

Mickey punched Jack's chest repeatedly as he lay on the floor. His body moved with the impact of each blow but there was no sign of life. Mickey heard the front door burst open but before he could get up the door to his front room opened wide

42

too. Jonny stood in the doorway, like a sinister silhouette in an old horror film. Mickey tried to breathe a sigh of relief but, choked up with saliva and tears, he could hardly breathe at all.

"What the fuck...?" he shouted at Mickey, who had got to his feet and stood trembling in the centre of the room.

Jonny walked into the room and stood in front of Mickey. Silent for a moment, he stared deep into his tear stained eyes. He took hold of Mickey's ears with both hands and shook his head firmly from side to side.

"Get a fuckin' grip! NOW!" he shouted.

He looked down at Jack and saw the blood soaked through his clothes. There was a smudge along the couch and a pool soaked into the carpet. It looked a lot, but Jonny had seen these scenes often enough to know that it always looked worse than it actually was.

"Grab his legs!" he ordered.

"What? No way!" cried Mickey.

"If you want a dead body for a fireside rug that's up to you, but if you don't," he paused, "GRAB HIS FUCKING LEGS!" he shouted.

Mickey, still crying, babbled something inaudible. He slumped slowly into action and grabbed Jacks' legs. Jonny hooked his hands under his shoulders and lifted. Mickey had neither the strength nor the inclination to lift Jack's legs off the floor.

"You better fuckin' do it!" ordered Jonny with wide eyes.

He lifted again and Mickey managed to get him elevated. The two of them carried the seemingly lifeless Jack out into the street to where Jonny had parked his car. Jack groaned as the coolness of the breeze wafted over him.

"He's still alive!" said Jonny, surprised and relieved.

Mickey became aware that he was out in the open, in the broad light of day, carrying a potential corpse. He dropped his legs in fright. He took a step back and covered his mouth with his hands. Jonny could see a dark patch around Mickey's groin and guessed that he had urinated at some time during the episode.

"Pick him the fuck up and get him in the car, you pathetic waste of DNA!" ordered Jonny in a sinister whisper, "Before anyone sees us!" he added.

Mickey cried loudly and shook his head, slowly at first but then faster. His nose was running and he slavered down his chin. He turned and ran back into his house.

"Am coming back to get you, Mickey!" he bellowed.

As the door slammed shut, Jack groaned again.

"I will get you, you fuckin' waster!" he added.

Jonny muttered and swore under his breath as he clumsily bundled Jack across the back seat of his car and jumped into the driver's seat. He sped off down the road with a screech of tyres and left two thin, black clouds of smoke behind him, gently dissipating into the air. As he rounded the corner of the Hospital and neared the main entrance he skidded to a halt, which immediately caught the attention of two nurses that were standing by the doorway. He waved and called to them as he jumped out of his car and they rushed over. They attracted the attention of a paramedic who appeared with a trolley and wheeled Jack through to Accident and Emergency. Jonny jogged next to the trolley as the nurses tried to take Jack's pulse.

"Don't you fuckin' die boy! Don't you dare fuckin' die!" he whispered.

One of the nurses, offended by the language although agreeing with the sentiment, scowled at him as they passed through two double doors. They slowed to a halt in an emergency ward, fully equipped with serious looking machines. An expert team of medics lifted Jack from the trolley and onto a bed in next to no time. All hands knew exactly where to be and what to do. Jonny stopped motionless as he entered the room, as if he had run into a barrier that would not allow him to pass. The seriousness of the situation and the intimidating sight of the life-saving equipment immediately overwhelmed him. He was ushered back out of the room and assured that the staff would do everything they possibly could to save Jack. The doors swung closed and Jonny stood staring through the small round windows with his empty mind and hollow legs failing to support him. He reached out for the wall and leaned with his head bowed.

Nursing staff surrounded Jack and attached pipes, tubes and wires to various parts of his upper body. It was seriously scary for Jonny. He did not know what to feel or think. He had not been in hospital under these circumstances before and although he gave the impression that he had no emotions, his reality was something quite different. If he could have found a mind to think about it, he would have been pleased there was nobody around to see him in his moment of weakness. One of the nurses had prepared a syringe and another had wired the fading patient up to one of the machines. A bedside monitor displayed Jack's vital signs as a nurse made careful notes.

"Can you tell me what happened, sir?" asked the nurse outside with Jonny, shattering his mental isolation.

"I dunno," he stuttered, "I found him in the street on my way to work."

The nurse looked at Jonny with a look that told him she knew he was lying. He broke away from her gaze and looked back through the window. A doctor had appeared with a defibrillator. Jonny turned back to the nurse. He did not know where to look or what to do. The hospital had crept into his psyche and was rapidly becoming a phobia. Sweat broke out across his forehead and his breathing became shallow. He had to be somewhere else, anywhere.

"Everything here is confidential, sir. Do you know who he is? Has he taken anything we should be made aware of?" the nurse pleaded reassuringly in a firm and focussed tone.

Jonny trembled and shook his head slowly. He turned to leave and repeated that he did not know Jack. He broke into a jog and then began running down the corridor and out into the open-air sanctuary of the world outside.

* * * * *

Rachel stepped off the bus with a polite 'thank you' to the driver and then paused in the street to check the numbers on the houses. Her stomach fluttered and she could not stop herself from smiling. The sound of excited young school children could be heard playing in the distance and somewhere in the streets beyond the houses, an ice cream van rang out its pleasant tune. The sounds of healthy youth provoked thoughts of how life should have been when Rachel was young; maybe if there had been more happiness in her childhood, she could have made better choices. Maybe she could have been another woman. Taking the first few steps towards reintroducing herself to her mother could change all that; this could be a fresh start.

Small semi-detached houses lined the street; most of them covered in pebbledash or pale shades of textured paint in various states of disrepair, with unkempt gardens. Here and there, dog dirt, weeds in cracks and litter in the gutters. Rachel battled with her optimism and tried hard to focus on the positive feelings she had rather than be dragged down by appearances. Eventually, with a disappointed sigh, she stopped at the end of a particularly overgrown garden. There was no gate on the post and the bin was lying in the long grass, which played host to many dandelions and thistles. Rachel took a letter out of her handbag, read the address again and looked up at the house in front of her. Slowly she walked, almost sulking, up the path towards the door. A piece of plywood had been used to replace one of the smaller side panes in the bay window. The curtains were filthy and hung at an angle but still managed to obscure the view into the house. Twice Rachel paused and stood motionless, staring at the door, trying to cling to some form of hope that this was the right thing to do and everything would go well. Her nerves played hell inside her and her doubts were taunting abuse.

When she had conquered her feelings and stood at the doorstep she took a deep breath before she knocked lightly. There was no reply so she knocked again a little louder. She hesitated as she made contact with the door, her stomach turning with a wave of a butterflies. Across at the window, there were no signs of life. She took a piece of paper out of her purse and scribbled her name and mobile phone number on it, along with the words, 'Please call me, it's important'. With a rusty squeak, she opened the letterbox and dropped the paper through just as a pale silhouette appeared behind the crinkled glass in the door and shouted,

"Who is it?" in a rough voice.

"I'm looking for Mrs Cooper; Mrs Sally Cooper,"

"What do you want? If it's money you can piss off!" she shouted.

The pale silhouette diminished as she turned to go.

"No, please," shouted Rachel as she knocked on the glass, "I've got good news! At least I think it is...!" she whispered to herself.

There was a momentary silence before the sound of a lock turning and a security chain dropping into place. The door squeaked as it opened slowly and a pale, wrinkled face peered out of the murk with narrow eyes.

"Who are you?" she demanded quickly.

"My name's Rachel Masters. I'm looking for Sally Cooper."

There was what Rachel thought a long, uncomfortable silence. She felt the tears welling up behind her eyes as the fluttering butterflies in her stomach had warped into clumsy moths. Her chest tightened and her breathing became difficult.

"I'm her daughter," she added.

The pause seemed to be longer and even more uncomfortable. Rachel had tried to restrain herself and not let her emotions get the better of her but she had to concede defeat. The tears started to sneak out of the corner of her eyes and her hands were shaking as she looked at the woman behind the door. Her eyes had narrowed as she squinted at Rachel.

"Sally doesn't live here, love. You better go!" said the woman.

"But wait... Do you know where she is?" pleaded Rachel as she stepped forward.

"No! Sod off!" the woman's voice was sharp as she retreated into her home and began to close the door.

"Please," wept Rachel as she pushed a trembling hand against the door, "where is she?"

"Get lost!" snapped the woman as she forced the door back into place.

Rachel turned and dropped herself down onto the doorstep. She sat with her head in her hands and cried. The surrounding tension had curved into sadness and held her in a lukewarm embrace. Her emotional landscape seemed to warp and distort, like a Salvador Dali painting. Had she crashed? Had her hopes fallen into the bowels of Hell? She certainly felt as if they had. Had she searched all her adult life for this? What had she ever done that made this fair?

Determined not to lose everything, she rubbed her eyes and face, and then stood up slowly. She walked down the street determined not to look back. The temptation to glance was growing with the distance she was putting between her and her disappointment although her anger and resilience held strong. She watched her feet through damp eyes as she walked quickly away from the house. The clicking sound of her heels seemed to grow louder in her ears until they joined in a rhythmic unison with her increasing heartbeat. Her anger grew and boiled up inside her. She felt hot beneath her coat. She was unaware that she had stormed out into a road until she heard the loud, sudden burst of a car horn coupled with the screech of brakes.

"Watch it, silly cow!" shouted a man from behind the wheel.

Rachel stopped suddenly and stood still in the middle of the road like a startled animal. She stared at the red-faced man leaning out of his car window.

"Well move then!" he moaned as he honked his horn again.

Rachel stared at him without any sign of emotion. She was not quite sure of where she was or what exactly was happening. She gathered her thoughts slowly as reality settled all around her and then raised her middle finger to him. She stomped off across the street and down towards the bus stop on the corner outside a newsagent's shop.

Chapter 3

Peter stepped out of the shower, took a towel from the nearby rail and wrapped it around his waist as he walked out from the steamy bathroom and into a large bedroom. He instantly located the flashing lights and familiar ringtone of his mobile phone, chirping from the bedside table and walked directly to it.

"Hello?"

He listened in silence for a few moments and then sat down on the bed. He ran his fingers through his hair and roughly combed it back off his face.

"OK. So she went to the Registry Office?" he questioned as he wiped his wet hand on his towel, "Do you think she's getting married?" he laughed, sarcastically.

He sat for a few minutes, nodding and making 'hmm' noises now and again. He stood up and headed back towards the bathroom.

"So you're sure of that? Even though you lost her? I'll tell what I think shall I?" he gesticulated with his free hand as his voice became steadily more angry.

"I think she's looking for someone. I think she went to the Registry Office to get details about that someone and to find out where they are now!" his voice grew louder and angrier.

"I think she's looking for me!" he shouted after a short pause.

He walked through to the kitchen and poured himself a cup of strong, black coffee as he spoke. Although the anger still welled up inside him, his voice began to calm down.

"She had a photo of someone I knew a long time ago. Somebody I thought I'd left behind!"

There was a short silence.

"So find out what she wanted with that registrar and how much she knows! I need answers and I need them now!"

He clicked the phone off and threw it across the room. It sailed out through the open door and into the living area. It landed with a bounce on the couch. He stared at the phone for a moment with the heat of his anger stirring inside him. He felt the onset of arousal and the need for release. He followed the phone through the same door and picked up the landline receiver from the wall by the door.

"Room service?" he asked in a very calm tone, "Special request: Can you send me up a maid please? Room 61. Can you send that young blonde? The European?"

* * * * *

"All right, all right, I'm coming!" shouted Mickey.

It had taken some time for Mickey to realise that the dull thudding sound he could hear was somebody knocking at his front door. He had been preoccupied for so long that it took some serious thought to remember where he was or what he was doing. It was as if he had been dreaming in a heavy sleep and the banging had woken him prematurely. Reluctantly, he stomped through his hallway to the front door carrying a floor cloth. It dripped as he walked, leaving a feint trail of dark red spots behind him. He reached out and flicked the lock open. The door immediately flung open with such a force that Mickey had to step back to avoid falling over.

"Wha...?" he stuttered, shocked.

Jonny pushed his way past Mickey and entered the living room.

"Told you I'd be back!" he warned in a sinister tone.

A young female with long, black hair with a bright pink fringe and heavy eye make-up followed him.

"All right, Mickey?" she hissed as she passed him.

Her big black boots padded with thick leather and heavy, metal buckles clumped loudly as she stomped across the floor. Her highly decorated leather jacket creaked quietly as she passed and filled the hall with a sweet odour of incense. Mickey followed cautiously into the room. The visitors had stood at the far end near the kitchen, with their backs to a window, which emphasised their ominous presence. Their silhouettes loomed like shadowy phantoms haunting in the half-light. He suddenly noticed how cold he felt and how heavy his eyelids were.

50

"What a mess!" said Jonny, nodding at the bloodstained carpet.

Mickey heard the voice from a distance, as if Jonny had spoken through a long tunnel and the words had spiralled towards him in a veil of intimidation.

"I'm cleaning up," stuttered Mickey holding up the leather cloth.

"Can't be much fun for you, Mickey. All this blood while you're stoned. How is he?" asked Jonny.

"I dunno," shrugged Mickey, "I haven't been."

"He had my brown!" said the girl.

Her voice boomed through the tunnel and headed straight for Mickey. Her tones whipped through his ears and struck him cold with fear.

"Sorry, Kit. I didn't know he was going to get hit!" shook Mickey.

"He had MY BROWN!" she repeated louder.

She flicked out her hand and a silver blade magically flashed into view. It sprung to life in the light from the window and glistened with a threatening shine. She took a couple of steps forward and Mickey took a couple back. Her blackness grew in his field of vision and obscured all sense of perspective. She raised the blade to his eye level and spun it through her fingers. She smiled with glee at her slight-of-hand skills and terrified Mickey with a narrow-eyed stare.

"You owe me, Mickey!" she whispered.

"I'm sorry Kit! I'll pay you back… honest… I will pay you back…" his voice trailed off as his legs emptied and could no longer support his weight.

Like a wave of wet cement, the feeling of the floor hitting his knees rolled up through his thighs and into his stomach. He felt an overwhelming urge to urinate and struggled not to. His skin felt as if it were two sizes too small and he instantly perspired from every pore. Kit turned to face Jonny and raised her hands with a loud laugh.

"He's such a fuckin' wimp, Jonny! Why do you put up with him?" she laughed.

Her words echoed in the vast emptiness of Mickey's ears and stung him to the core. Jonny shrugged his shoulders in silence. Kit swiftly turned to face Mickey. Like a scared child beneath a duvet trying in vain to hide from the monster beneath the bed, he raised his cloth in front of him. His bottom lip quivered as Kit walked slowly closer to him. She crouched slightly forward and narrowed her eyes. With the delicate grace of a ballet dancer she spread her arm out wide and held the knife in front of her with the other hand. Slowly, with deliberate intimidation, she approached, like a big black spider creeping up on a doomed fly. Mickey staggered back on his knees until he felt his feet hit the couch. He stopped suddenly and dropped his eyes to the floor. She tucked the sharp point of her blade in the notch beneath his chin and pushed his face up to look him in the eye. She paused just long enough for Mickey to begin sobbing again. He shook his head slowly and felt the sharp point of the blade rubbing against his chin without breaking the flesh. She turned to look at Jonny and stood up straight. With an unnaturally smooth movement of her arm she dropped the knife back into her pocket.

"You will pay back every fuckin' penny!" she hissed.

She turned quickly and kicked Mickey in the chest. He felt the weight of her boots travel through his body and he was incapable of stopping his momentum. He fell awkwardly against the couch, rolled sideways and splayed out across the floor in the puddle of bubbles and blood that he had been working on earlier. Jonny laughed and he walked towards Kit. They interlocked in a deep, passionate kiss and then quietly left the room.

"48 hours and counting!" she shouted to him as she pulled the front door closed behind her.

* * * * *

Rachel stared at the display on her mobile phone with a scowl. The number that had been calling her intermittently throughout the course of the morning was 'Withheld'. She had come to hate that word. She stared at the screen as if it would give her some clue, but it just became the focus of her frustration. She slammed the phone into her handbag with an agitated sigh and continued shopping. Normally, she was not so wound up and would not have become so stressed about such calls; probably a shy punter, wanting her services but too afraid to ask. It happened a lot. She still had the parasitic emptiness wallowing in her, feeding on her sadness, reminding her that her mother was lost and the search had been fruitless. It was a parasite that toyed with her moods and she was in no fit state for games with unknown clients.

Dave watched from a discreet distance. He had found a suitable place to sit where he had a panoramic view of the shopping arcade. He watched her as she shopped, being sure that the doors he could see were the only ones in and out of the row of retail outlets opposite him. He sat on the bench with arms stretched out confidently over the backrest and his legs crossed in front of him. It was unseasonably pleasant for the time year and he felt surprisingly relaxed. Usually, Peter would have him threatening business rivals or roughing up some poor unfortunate that could not repay a debt, but this job was an easy ride. The money was better than usual and the client was apparently harmless, not to mention incredibly beautiful, which made watching her a real pleasure.

He looked on in admiration as she walked along the arcade. Her legs and her fine figure were enticing and inviting. She stopped suddenly, dipped into her handbag again and pulled out her phone with an excited smile. He could see her mouth the word 'hello' several times before she dropped it back into her bag with a frustrated frown. She turned and stormed into a large department store at the end of the row. Dave remembered that there were several other exits to that shop so he jumped up quickly and trotted after her. As he neared the shop he slowed down and entered casually. He took his time and held the door for two older women that followed him in, all the while he kept his eye on his prize across the shop floor. He smiled to the women and casually continued his pursuit. In the clothes department, he spied on Rachel from a parallel aisle and kept a discreet eye on her from over the rails of expensive outfits. He pretended to admire the clothes, feeling the cloth and looking at the price tags like any other shopper in the building.

"Jesus! For that?" he whispered as he saw the price tag on a simple silk blouse.

A shopping assistant within earshot frowned and tutted at him disapprovingly. Rachel dipped into her handbag for her phone again and paused a while before she said 'hello'. She hesitated as she listened to the handset. She concentrated hard on the feint hissing as she tried to make out some background noise that may give her a clue as to who was calling her.

"Hello?" croaked a voice at the other end of the phone.

"Hello?" replied Rachel quickly.

She recognised the voice as the lady she had met yesterday.

"Is that you? Is that Rachel?"

"Yes," she replied shakily.

"I've got some news about your mother. Can you come round?"

Rachel felt her legs empty and her knees wobble. She reached out to a clothing rail and held on for balance. Her smile lit up her face and she gasped with delight as the old woman spoke. She breathed deeply before she answered.

"I'm coming now!" she said in an excited voice, "I'm on my way right now!"

Quickly, she dropped the phone back in her bag and turned to leave the shop, running through the make-up department and out of the exit towards the bus station. She walked trotted towards the bus stop as she scanned the electronic displays on the front of the buses. With an optimistic smile, she found the name she was looking for and ran towards the stop. Unfortunately, the bus pulled out and drove away before she had a chance to get near. She walked slower with a frown on her face as she headed towards the shelter to wait for the next bus. Dave watched her from the edge of the station and saw where she had gone. He walked around the periphery of the station to avoid her line of sight. He joined the queue of people behind her. It was several minutes before the next bus arrived.

Rachel paid her fare and went upstairs. Dave sat downstairs close to the exit so he could remain inconspicuous and see when she got off. The bus was not full but there were enough people on board to blend in amongst. He did not feel so obvious seated with other passengers, but he became more and more uncomfortable as the bus eventually emptied. After quite some time he had travelled a fair distance into a housing estate on the edge of town when his doubts started plaguing his thoughts. He began to think that maybe she had slipped by him and he had lost her. But how could that have happened? She would have to pass right under his nose to get off the bus. Maybe she got off a couple of stops ago with a group of people; she could have hidden behind someone.

No sooner had he thought himself into believing that she had given him the slip than she appeared at the bottom of the stairs. Her high heels were not the best match for the bumpy ride on the bus as she staggered her way towards the exit. The bus pulled over and she stepped out into the street with an unshakeable blend of determination and optimism. Dave waited for the next stop just a couple of hundred metres down the road and then he got off too. He walked swiftly back along the street and soon saw Rachel in the distance walking towards him. He saw her pause then turn into a garden so he increased his pace and began to jog. When he arrived at the garden gate, the front door closed. Reaching into his coat pocket and pulled out his phone.

"Carl? I've found her. I'll snoop around and see what I can see. I'm on…" he paused as he wandered up the road a short distance looking for a road sign, "…Cornwall Avenue, on the Manor Garth estate. You go in and check out the flat. Have a rummage but keep it clean. We don't want her knowing we've been there. That means no souvenirs! D'you hear me? Find out what you can. Call me when you're out."

* * * * *

Rachel stood in the hallway with her stomach somersaulting and her legs feeling hollow. She felt her cheeks warm and her eyes well up with tears.

"You know where my mother is?" she stammered, "Are you a friend? A relative?"

"I got the note you left me," she croaked, ignoring Rachel's questions.

Rachel followed the woman down a stale smelling hall into a dirty kitchen where every available space had used crockery or pans in it. They turned into the living room and the smell of wet dog blended with whiskey hit Rachel like a dull thud of stagnant air. Taken aback by the smell, she stopped in her tracks before she stepped any further into the room. The woman had sat down in an armchair by the window. She reached out and switched the radio off. Rachel walked into the centre of the room not knowing what to do or say.

"Sit down, love," offered the woman.

"Do you know my mother?" asked Rachel with a weepy voice.

She was hardly able to contain her excitement and shuffled her feet beneath her.

"Aye. I do," she replied without any hint of emotion.

Rachel fell into the couch and sunk down into the well-worn cushions. She began to cry and wiped her eyes with her hands. She sat undisturbed for what felt like several minutes. The woman raised a bottle of whiskey and poured herself a glass. She picked up a packet of cigarettes, lit one for herself and flicked the packet in Rachel's direction.

"Want a fag?" she asked.

Rachel, still crying, shook her head and wiped her cheek with the back of her hand. She looked down at the floor, which appeared coated in a layer of grey-green grime set hard by the passing of time.

"Where is my mum?" she trembled.

"I'm here love!" she swigged the whiskey down in one gulp and plonked the glass on the small table beside her chair, "I'm Sally Cooper."

Silence. The only sound was the feint ticking of a small clock. A pause in time held the two women together, second by second. Sally broke the still,

"Never thought I'd see you again, though. Not after they took you off me," she leaned forward in her chair.

"But when I came..." Rachel began.

"I couldn't see you then! You showing up out of the blue! I didn't know what to do! They sent me letters, you know, the adoption people but I didn't know what to do about it. They use big words and small writing on them fancy computers these days and I just didn't get it!"

"I'm sorry," Rachel wept, "I didn't think. I assumed you had agreed to meet with me. I thought they wouldn't give me your address unless you agreed?"

"I don't think they should o'done, love, but never mind. You're here now. You want a drink?" Sally offered.

Rachel shook her head. She pulled her purse out of her handbag and looked long and hard at the photograph. At long last the woman in the faded picture sat opposite her, although she found it very difficult to see any resemblance. She offered the picture to Sally with a hopeful smile.

"I've been holding on to this for years," she said gently, "looking for you. Hoping to find you."

Sally pulled a pair of well-worn spectacles out from between the cushions of her chair and scrutinised the photo as Rachel explained who she was and how she had come to find her mother after all these years. She told her all about her childhood; how she had been passed from one well-meaning foster carer to the next until she was old enough to get her own flat. Sally listened between pouring more whiskey and swigging each glass back in a single gulp. She stared at Rachel with swaying eyes and a wobble in her posture. Sally picked up the photo again and held it up to the light.

"That's not you, you know?" she said knowing that Rachel believed it was.

"What?" Rachel was shocked; "It's got to be! It's me as a baby and you before you left me! It's me and you!"

"It's not, love. Sorry!" she spoke slowly with an almost caring tone.

In an instant Rachel's hopes had vanished and left her with nothing but an empty space, wrapped in doubt and confusion. That creased old photograph had been the driving force of her life for as long as she could remember. All the nights of crying herself to sleep in beds she didn't want to be in while holding on to that picture and the feint hope that her mother was out there, somewhere, waiting. All the times she had stared into the woman's eyes and wished she had known her. All her dreams fell to her feet like a sodden sack of dead kittens.

"No. You were very ill when you were born. You were tiny and twisted. Doctors reckoned you might die!" she swaggered back into her chair.

"They took you from me very early on. Straight away, give or take. You went into the special care unit and had wires and all sorts in you for months. I never saw you again. That baby on the photo is your brother!" she said with her eyes closed.

Rachel absorbed the moment and wished that she did not have to. She felt nauseous, shocked and dizzy.

"You're a twin. He was a big baby and got the lion's share of me! He robbed you in the womb, so they said, and you got ill," her speech slurred and she yawned aloud, "You didn't know that did you?" she asked, leaning forward again and pouring another drink.

"No…" wept Rachel.

The miserable thought of the baby not being her outweighed the delight that she had finally found her mother. Rachel did not recognise the emotion she was feeling. It was discordant, unbalanced and putrid. The two sat in silence again, the only sounds being Rachel's gentle weeping and the glug-glug of the pouring whiskey, drowning out the delicate ticking of the little clock.

Rachel was absorbed into her anxieties, fighting against a tumultuous tirade of uncertainty. Her cutting thoughts clouded her mind. Sally flicked the radio on and listened thoughtfully as if Rachel was not there. She stared into the middle distance without moving save for that of the tiny rocking motion caused by a sudden onset of hiccups.

"Who is he?" asked Rachel quietly after a long, uncomfortable pause.

There was no response from Sally.

"Who is he?" she said a little louder.

"Eh? Who? Your brother?"

Rachel saw that Sally had drifted off and for a moment she was unaware of the happenings in the room. With a shake of her head and a shrug, she turned to Rachel,

"James Edward Cooper," she said with pride, "They took him off me when he was three. When I started to drink. They didn't like that, the social and the doctors, you know," she waved her hands at Rachel.

"They said I was unfit! Bastards! What did they know? I had 'issues', according to them do-gooders. Most of 'em were only kids 'emselves, not parents! How dare they tell me I had issues!" her voice conveyed her distrust and hatred.

Rachel sat upright in the couch, trying not to touch too much of it for fear of getting the grime and smell onto her expensive clothes. Thousands of thoughts had started to settle in her mind like grubby little snowflakes. This filthy woman was her mother. Why did she live in such squalor? What had happened to make her like this? Surely this could not be the affect that losing her children had had on her after all these years.

"Have you found your Father? Doubt you ever will!" she laughed, "He was a very devious bastard!" she slurred with a sour voice and her eyes narrowed.

Rachel was taken aback. Her eyes widened and she took a sharp intake of breath. An action she immediately regretted when she realised that she had gulped in a noticeable amount of the stale air. She recoiled slightly and coughed in her throat.

"He had a lot of unsavoury friends, he did," she spoke quietly, her voice interrupted by her hiccups, "Probably dead by now. Stabbed in the back by someone he shit on!"

Sally shuffled in her seat and looked as if she might cry for a moment, but then, with a loud sigh, she blinked hard a few times and turned to Rachel.

"We went out together for two years. That was a bloody long time for me back then! I was young and foolish. I didn't know any better," she swigged another glass of whiskey and attempted to pour another dram but the bottle was empty.

Sally struggled up to her feet, reached out to the wall for support and slowly staggered herself through to the kitchen. Rachel could see that the wallpaper at that height had started to wear thin and pale grey grime overdubbed its original pattern. Sally had obviously used that wall as a support for many years. Rachel sat and reflected on the echoing statements running through her mind. She wrestled with the reality of her mother's life as she compared it to the fantasy she had created as she was growing up. The two people, the mother and the fantasy mother, were as different as it was possible to be. This was not as Rachel had imagined it to be at all. Everything was wrong. As Rachel wrangled with her thoughts, Sally reappeared with another bottle and fell into her chair.

"We split up because I fell in love with one of his mates. We started having an affair behind his back. I was too scared to leave him straight away because he might do something nasty. I was planning on letting him down slowly, you know? But your father found out. He took him fishing, pretending he didn't know about us, and he killed him!" she began to weep.

Rachel was shocked. She jolted inside, like a hammer of something heavy had suddenly dropped like a dead weight through her whole body. Hearing stories of murder was nothing new to Rachel. In her line of work she had met some very dubious characters that had felt the need to tell her all kinds of unimaginable secrets. She felt it was part of her service, a necessary evil in some cases, to keep quiet and listen. She was the only confidant some men had in their lives and she allowed them the opportunity to unload. She never did anything with the information; in fact she hardly paid it any real attention at all, and she never, under any circumstances whatsoever, asked questions. She was well aware that her lifestyle meant that she lived close enough to serious crime to smell it, taste it or even touch it if she reached out a little. She respected the distance and kept it as best she could, but her mother's disclosure had made such things a part of her heritage, and that distance had closed.

"He drugged him up to his eyeballs and threw him out the boat. He drowned him in the lake. Your father told me all about it."

Rachel shuffled in her seat; the discomfort caused by the muck and the grime seemed irrelevant now. The shocking revelation had put things into perspective. Rachel struggled with her thoughts of having an alcoholic mother and a murderous father. She was beginning to wish she had never embarked on her mission to find her mother. This search had affected her life for years. Throughout her childhood, she had developed wondrous stories to support her mother's absence. During her adolescence she had started to find out how to go about finding her again. In her early twenties she had made contact with the adoption agencies and the authorities to get the information she required. All the while, her behaviour and life choices reflected her loss and displayed her anger towards the world. Her inability to form long-term relationships, her distrust of caring and her deep-rooted, subliminal bitterness, all affected her personal development. She became ever more aware of her negative attributes as she aged and decided that the symptoms were no longer easy to treat. The only cure was to confront the root cause and find her mother. Now her search was complete and, theoretically, they could start all over again.

At least Rachel thought it should be so straight forward, but her mother was now adding to the complications. New layers of history revealed, like a false summit beckoning the mountaineer to the peak, only to reveal a higher climb beyond. Sally fought hard to keep her eyes open as she turned towards Rachel and pointed.

"When he came home, he told me what he'd done. He beat me up. Then he raped me. That's how you and your brother came about. I know that 'cause it's the only time we did it without a condom on!"

Rachel was wide eyed and fixed her stare at Sally. Sally bobbed her head up and down a little as she struggled to keep her eyes open. Both of the Rachel's she could see wavering in front of her were paying attention. Rachel was riveted. Her parentage was not at all as she had hoped. She had conjured up some negative scenarios about why her parents gave her up, just in case she would be disappointed, but this was far beyond imaginable.

"I was going to abort, but I didn't have it in me. Then when you were born, how could I not love you? Babies are powerful creatures you know. They can change people's lives just like that!"

Sally clicked her fingers in front of her with a great deal of effort and very little sound. She had started to nod intermittently as she began drifting off to sleep. She jolted her head up and tried hard to open her eyes but eventually the battle was lost. Sally slumped back in her chair and fell into a deep alcohol induced sleep.

All her preparation, based on an idyllic fantasy, now utterly destroyed by a exceedingly harsh reality, dazed Rachel. She had become lost. Her insides felt empty, like hunger, only not for food. She was warm, yet not comfortable. There was a small element of disgust and repulsion in her body language and her face turned down, as if she were about to vomit. She stared at the sleeping Sally and slowly got up to her feet. She walked through to the kitchen and out into the hall where she stood motionless and stared at nothing. Time had become separate and had no meaning. She could have stood there for a minute, an hour or all day. It made no difference; the duration was irrelevant; unknown. She walked back into the kitchen then back into the hall, her thoughts in tune with the sounds of her footsteps, changing from clicks on the cold kitchen tiles to gentle thuds on the softer hall carpet.

Confusion steered her mind and her thoughts confused her actions. Her world swept up in a whirlwind that swirled around her, random, chaotic and in disarray. She stood alone in the eye of her storm, desperately trying to find a constructive course along this pessimistic path to self-destruction that Sally had been walking for years. She reached out without thinking and opened a door. It was a storage cupboard with an electricity meter partially obscured behind a clotheshorse and a vacuum cleaner. Inspiration flashed across her thoughts like the saving rays of a lighthouse as she slowly realised what she was looking at. She tried another door and found the toilet. The smell was unbearable. The carpet had faded into several shades of yellow and green and there were some toadstools growing in a damp corner. Rachel was almost sick.

She turned to the hall and headed for the front door. She pulled it wide and wedged it open with a folded newspaper from a pile of old junk mail she found on the floor. She stood in the frame and inhaled deeply from the air outside. It was cool, fresh and a welcome relief to the fusty atmosphere in the house. She walked through to the kitchen and looked around. She opened the back door too and propped it open with the over-flowing bin. She opened as many windows as she could throughout the downstairs of the house. She went through the hall again and went upstairs. Strangely, the rooms were in a much better condition. There was a lot of dust on the surfaces but no grease or grime. In one of the bedrooms, a large black Labrador had curled up at the foot of the bed. It looked around slowly and then went back to sleep, seemingly uninterested in the unknown visitor. Across the hall, the second bedroom was quite tidy, if a little musty, with a television set and a large double wardrobe. The bathroom was quite clean, although the taps and plugholes were dry enough to indicate they had not been used for a long, long time. The air smelled cold and dry.

Rachel took some tissue from the roll and wiped around the seat before she used the toilet. As she sat on the cold plastic, she thought. It became obvious to Rachel that Sally had not been upstairs for quite some time and had been living in the downstairs rooms. She reaffirmed with herself that she would like to become a part of Sally's life and would start by getting her house back in order. Before she went downstairs, she gathered up a thick woollen blanket from one of the beds. She went through to the room where Sally was sleeping and checked that she was comfortable. She carefully covered her to keep her warm against the fresh air coming in from outside. When she was certain she was warm, in no danger of choking or falling out of her chair, she switched off the radio and removed the bottle from her side. Sally grunted and shuffled beneath the blanket but remained sleeping.

Rachel strolled out into the street with a subtle sense of achievement. She consoled herself with the thought that she had at least found her mother and the two of them had met. It was a positive meeting in as much as she was not rejected, which before the shocking revelations, was her biggest fear. Rachel began to focus on the positives rather than the negatives, although she found it very difficult not to think about the alcohol abuse and the alleged murder. She strode down to the corner shop with a smile. As she walked, the fresh air filled her lungs. The coolness refreshed her skin and her thoughts become brighter. The despair that she had slumped into was fading, slowly but surely. She began to feel a kind of warmth she had not felt before, a family kind of belonging, a hopeful kind of happiness.

Within the hour, she returned to the house with two carrier bags filled with cleaning products and various accessories. She entered the hallway with a determined gait, placed the bags down in front of her, threw her coat over the end of the banister and rolled up her blouse sleeves. Her mission to save her mother started here.

* * * * *

Peter stood at the head table as he addressed his selected audience of local councillors and high-profile businessmen. He appeared to have them captivated with his professional blend of humour and precise detail relative to the plan that he was presenting. The obedient wives and pleasure-seeking girlfriends smiled constantly and giggled at all the right times whenever the opportunity arose. Peter thought that their white lace frills and fake diamonds betrayed their lack of elegance and gave a false impression of style. He distrusted most women and hated the fickle ones. Above all, he despised those that were so eager to please that they would live a lie in order to steal a higher standard of living from their dumb husband's fat wallets. Peter likened it to dishonest prostitution, selling their bodies for material goods without realising or admitting what they were actually doing.

Here and there, single people perched like hungry vultures on the edges of their seats made suggestive nods and slight smiles to each other. The flirting flew between the tables, lingering on chests, on legs, on faces. Peter could see the games being played from the front of the room. He had the hosts' eye view of the charged atmosphere, dripping with want, wealth and power. He knew the games people played and he used it to his advantage. His psychological overview gave him the upper hand and inflated his superiority complex. All eyes were on Peter.

"When the lottery funding is granted in the coming weeks, I will be looking to you for further investment to make this the most successful rehabilitation project this side of the River!" Peter raised his hands to a ripple of applause, "and so, to a new horizon; a new beginning, my friends and colleagues," he raised a Champaign glass, "To Newbury Hall!"

"Newbury Hall!" they chanted in unison as they too raised their glasses.

Peter knew he was the puppet master and looked at the theatre of mindless marionettes staring back at him with inflexible grins and nodding heads. His wealth and entrepreneurship had established him as the alpha male among this pack of ravenous scavengers. Most of the fools at the feast only had a vague idea of what Peter had been talking about for the last thirty-five minutes or so but they all pretended to be impressed and 'on board' with the scheme.

The wealthy businessmen rocked back and forth in their matching suits and chauvinistic attitudes with well-timed quips and comments. They used specific, interesting words and phrases in long-winded monologues that never really said anything. Whole conversations could take place and get nowhere, in the same academic way that politicians wax lyrical but still manage to avoid actually answering a question. The business talk was enough to switch off the most curious of ears.

Peter, unimpressed but never revealing himself as so, took his seat beside a beautiful blonde girl as his colleagues clapped him a small round of applause. She was wearing a pale evening dress with a diamond necklace and nothing else, which became obvious to anyone that allowed their gaze to linger over her fine figure. She seemed a little uneasy in the company of these highly educated rich people, not only because of her obvious language differences but also because of their ignorance and arrogance. She shuffled in her seat and smiled at Peter, not really sure of how best to behave. She looked up to him with sheepish eyes, almost apologetically,

"It is a good reception, no?" she questioned with a forced smile and a heavy accent.

"Oh yes, very good. They all agree it's a top idea and it should give them a good return," Peter replied as he stroked her cheek with the back of his finger.

Annelise felt a chill roll down her spine as he touched her. She remembered her experience earlier in the room upstairs where she had to force him away from her, as he became too aggressive for her liking. She didn't mind selling herself for extra money but she didn't like it rough. Peter noticed her flinch and gave her a look that made her feel even colder. For a moment, the fear in her eyes interested Peter and he felt a warmth flash through his cheeks. She excused herself and left the table.

"Powder her nose!" Peter smiled to his nearest colleague.

"She's a beauty, Peter. I bet she wasn't cheap!" he nodded.

"On the contrary, James, she's just another maid at the Hotel. I offered her a little extra to dine with me this evening," Peter smiled again and sipped his Champaign, "I doubt she's even legal!" he added with a laugh.

The guests at the head table were discussing how their own organisations would be involved with various aspects of the Newbury Hall plan. They jostled with each other through conversations as they tried to out-do their associates. Several of the companies represented at the reception were financial backers; astute business associates that were willing to throw money at a sound investment. Peter knew the most influential and powerful proprietors in the region, and several of their darkest secrets. It was this splendid combination of knowledge that allowed him to encourage their involvement in many of his schemes, even if at first they may not have appreciated the full benefits. However, on this occasion, it seemed a very sensible idea to open a drug rehabilitation centre at the heart of the city to enhance Peter's existing programme that had been doing so well over recent years. There were more than enough drug-users in the area and the numbers were increasing. The health services in the county were all facing debts and failing to reach the government targets. The fruits of the forest were ripe for the picking.

The Champagne kept flowing and the conversations turned smutty. The evening was getting late and the guests had started to couple up. Peter remembered his companion, but when he looked about the room she had gone. He had assumed that she had been mingling with the guests and meeting people on his behalf, as he had requested when he hired her for the evening. Subsequently, he wondered what had happened to Annelise. She must not have returned from powdering her nose three hours ago. Peter was angry that he was without company on his most important evening after he had paid her a considerable sum of money. He made his polite excuses to his colleagues within earshot and meandered his way slowly to the toilets. He stopped only fleetingly to ask the bar staff clearing the tables if they had seen Annelise.

"Excuse me, Miss?" he asked politely, "Would you please go into the ladies to see if my friend is in there? I'd go myself but…" he smiled and shrugged his shoulders.

"OK, no problem," she replied.

Peter waited outside for a moment. He tapped his fingers against the doorframe and sighed.

"No one in there," she shrugged.

"OK," he paused and turned away before he paused again, "I don't suppose you…?" he started, looking over his shoulder.

"What...?" she questioned back.

"No, no. It's a silly idea. You wouldn't want to," he turned away again.

"Try me."

"Exactly!" he smiled as he turned to face her.

She smiled a wide smile and took a step closer to him.

"I've got a job to do here but when I'm finished I could meet you at the bar if you like?" she ran her fingers down his tie provocatively, as if to sweeten the deal.

"I would like that very much," he smiled and gently touched her elbow.

Peter returned to his colleagues in the dining area and took his time to talk to the small groups of friends that had gathered together in cliques on various tables. He impatiently wasted the remaining hours of the night in pointless small-talk conversations with people in various states of intoxication. Some of the women flirted with him and he took full advantage of the situation. He discreetly fondled buttocks when the opportunity arose and tried his best to touch the women as often as possible without appearing to be doing it deliberately. He felt powerful in the thought that he could have taken any of the women up to his room with him, if he wanted, and they would have loved to. They were as putty in his hands, but alas, for the poor, unfortunate women left in the hall, Peter considered them too old, too plump and just not attractive enough.

At last, the guests had dwindled and all that remained were those awkward men that did not manage to couple with anyone. They were either too engrossed in conversations about their own mini-empires or they were just too drunk to hold a half-decent conversation with an interested woman. Peter dismayed at these people. They had education and wealth but still he considered them to be wasting their precious little lives away. The waitress he had spoken with earlier was standing at the bar sipping her drink. She beckoned him over. He walked quickly, but not so quickly that he gave the impression he was desperate.

"What's your name?" he asked.

"Claire," she replied.

Peter ordered a shot of bourbon and gulped it down as Claire finished her drink. Without talking he took her by the hand and walked her over to the lift. They fell in through the doors and embraced in a passionate kiss until they arrived at their floor. Claire was taken aback by the suddenness of the advances but she chose not to resist, after all, this man was very wealthy, and that gave him a free reign as far as this waitress on minimum wage was concerned. They walked quickly through the dimly lit corridor towards Peter's room. Annelise, in her navy blue maid's uniform, stopped in the corridor as the two approached her. She looked like a harbinger of doom in the soft mood lighting. She stared at Claire with a frightened look on her face. She glanced at Peter and lowered her eyes.

"Ignore her," whispered Peter, "she's jealous!"

The look on Annelise's face alarmed Claire. She looked away from the maid who was now shaking her head slowly and whispering what sounded like a warning in a foreign language. Claire could not help but give her one last look and she immediately wished that she had not. Something in her eyes disturbed her and made her stomach turn. She swallowed hard and tried to shake the image from her mind as Peter slid his card through the lock and the lights turned green. As the door closed behind them, they embraced again. Peter undressed quickly while Claire watched.

"What you playing at, Tiger?" she smiled.

"No time for small talk! We both know why we're here. Just get undressed and get busy!" he said impatiently, as he threw his clothes across the floor.

"Hmmm. Like to get straight to the point do you?" she said as she started to lower her skirt.

Peter sat naked on the bed. He looked up at Claire as she undressed slowly. His erection was so hard he felt as if it would burst. He became more and more impatient for her as she swayed her hips slowly in font of him. He punched the bed with one hand and held his erection in the other.

"Come on girl!" he said quickly.

"Patience!" she whispered as she continued to dance seductively with her patterned lace bra peeking through her unbuttoned white cotton blouse. She leaned forward and licked her lips.

"Fuck this!" he said, as he jumped up.

He grabbed her by the shoulders and spun her round to lay her on the bed. She fell back hard and bounced a little on the firm mattress. At first she smiled and showed him her teeth with a humorous growl, but her face took on a different expression when he tore away her lace panties. He ripped them away so violently that he scratched her legs with his nails. She screamed a little and then pleaded,

"Slow down, man, what's the problem?" with a feint hint of fear in her voice.

Peter slapped her hard across the face and grabbed her by the throat. He pushed her knee aside with his free hand and thrust himself into her.

"Get off!" she growled through her squashed vocal chords as she tried hard to push him away.

She could feel the pain of him thrusting into her dry vagina. The friction stung and she began to cry out for him to stop. She slapped, kicked and rocked her body as much as she could from beneath him. She could feel the heat becoming more intense between her legs. The grip on her throat was so tight that her struggling made it increasingly difficult for her to breathe. Peter pinned her down with his hands on her upper arms and his body-weight above her. Her attacks were futile and served only to anger him more, which he seemed to enjoy. He slapped her again. He withdrew and gathered her up in his arms.

"You fuckin' love it!" he growled as he pulled her head back by her hair.

He threw her down face first and dropped his weight onto her back. Claire was kicking and punching in vain. Her screams were mere whimpers, buried in the duvet. He forced himself inside her again. This time the heat had subsided and she had become warm and moist. She knew she was bleeding. Punching and kicking, she bounced her body in an attempt to loosen his grip of her. He pinned her down again, pressing down on her shoulders so that her screams faded into the mattress. Claire's fear heightened her strength and she managed to spin herself over and push him off her for a moment. Peter, shocked at her disobedience, punched her in the jaw and she flopped back onto the mattress, lifeless and limp. He threw her round and grabbed her by the throat. Her head was hanging back over the foot of the bed. He pulled down her chin and thrust his penis into her mouth. Claire came round slowly and realised what was happening to her. She could taste the bitterness of his sweat mixed with her own blood. She could feel the heat of his penis in her mouth and his scrotum smothered against her nose. In the absence of oxygen she had become disorientated and delirious. She saw a vision of the blonde maid in the shadows of the room, praying to her, trying to warn her. Claustrophobic waves gripped her panicked mind. She muffled a scream in the depths of her throat. She bit down hard. He felt her teeth scratch at the shaft and stretch his already pulsating penis to its limit like elastic at the end of its reach.

Peter screamed and withdrew quickly. He jumped into the light of the en-suite bathroom as if fired from a gun. He panicked as he hopped up and down, holding his painful penis, fighting with the nightmare of what he might find when he looked at his damaged manhood. It burned. Although his flesh was red with abrasions, his skin had not been broken and the only blood on his genitals seemed to be hers. The wave of relief was almost overwhelming. He stormed angrily back into the bedroom but Claire had gone.

The corridor swirled as she ran. The heat between her legs and the pain throughout her pelvis seemed to increase with her sprinting. Unaware of which way she was running, she felt knotted, violated and destroyed. She had twisted her neck and pulled a muscle in her shoulder. The pain and heat between her legs became indistinguishable from extreme cold. She was empty and alone. Faster and faster, without forethought, without looking back, she ran.

A confusion of thoughts crossed her mind. What happened? Why? Her body seemed to disappear with an absence of feeling and she became nothing more than a collection of thoughts in a wide-open space, like a shoal of frightened fish in the deepest, darkest ocean. Fear gripped her. Oblivious to her own appearance and all other happenings in the corridor, she ran as fast as her pain would allow until she eventually burst through the double doors and into the service stairwell. She clumsily jumped down each flight of six steps to the landings in order to get away as quickly as she could. She seemed unhindered by her bare feet thudding on the cold hard concrete of the stairs. She bounced off the walls and fell through the final doorway, all the time hurtling faster and more furiously towards the sanctuary of her own room.

Chapter 4

Rachel awoke with a smile and an unusual eagerness to rise. She felt so enthused that she wanted to jump out of bed the instant her eyes had opened, but her body did not want to leave her comfortable sanctuary. She snuggled herself into her feather pillows with a contented sigh. Most mornings when she found herself at home she felt as if she wanted to hide beneath her duvet and never surface. Even though she seldom woke up in it, she loved her own bed. More often than not she woke up in unfamiliar beds when she had stayed out working, but this was no ordinary morning. This was a morning filled with hope and expectation. Today she felt as if she was a part of a family, just as she had always wished. She sang her way through her morning routine as she washed and dressed.

The day was no brighter than any other crisp autumn day but Rachel felt as if spring had sprung and everything was going her way. She had dealt with her disappointment about her mother and had accepted that her father was of dubious character. She did not know if she could believe everything Sally had told her considering her alcohol dependency, although she had accepted that there was probably an element of truth in there somewhere. Regardless of past history, Rachel was considering herself a part of a family now. She was no longer an orphan.

The relief of finding the elusive woman in the photograph had strengthened her emotional wellbeing and made her life's ambition worthwhile. Momentarily, she considered how devastated she would have been had she not found her at all and shuddered. She had spent a long time talking with Sally and the two of them had made a good start on their relationship. Rachel had cleaned the house thoroughly while she and Sally shared stories and got to know each other. However tentative the conversations may have been, the awkward silent spaces were soon entered into by the two eager women, willing to try, to share and to begin afresh. Rachel had provided Sally with a reason to reduce her drinking and take a more positive outlook on life; being a mother.

They had spoken about many things, not least Rachel's brother, and the day had ended positively with a goodbye hug. Rachel remembered that hug with a smile and a warm heart. Today was the day that Rachel was going to find her brother too; she just knew it. She hummed her way around the kitchen as she made herself tea and toast and then got herself ready to venture out into the world. She had her brother's birth details and had made another appointment at the Registry Office.

"James Edward," she thought to herself, "what a grand sounding name. I wonder what he does for a living?"

She pottered around her house, biding her time pointlessly with trivialities in order to keep her occupied and burn off some of her nervous excitement. She ensured that she had switched off her work mobile and ignored the flashing red light on her answerphone; no clients were going to interrupt her today. Her mind roamed far and wide, creating a life and a history for her unknown brother. She tried to think of all the positive life choices he should have made while she was struggling with the bad decisions that had led her to her present state of affairs. She imagined him in the armed forces, a handsome man in a uniform, someone that could really make his mother proud. The thought crossed her mind that if he was a military man, stationed abroad, in Iraq or Afghanistan and she may never trace him. She shook the unsettling thought out of her mind and decided that he would have a family of his own and a respectable job in an office, somewhere on the industrial estate or the new development near the docks. She felt sure he had settled in suburbia with a mortgage and a health plan. The fantasy filled her with hope and drew a full smile across her face until she beamed with happiness. She felt so good that she could not stop herself smiling. She was still humming to herself through her smile when she arrived at the Registry Office.

Dave had been waiting outside Rachel's flat in his car with Carl when she left. He had followed her briskly on foot through the same streets she had walked down the last time he tried to keep up with her. When she arrived at her destination, a wedding ceremony had just finished in another room and the waiting area was full of guests getting ready to leave. Dave made himself comfortable among the seated gathering and opened up a daily newspaper. He sat in the waiting area, next to the heavy, ornate wooden door, slightly ajar. With a strained effort, he was as close to being within earshot of the office as he could get. As he read the paper and admired the topless models, he thought about Rachel and wondered why Peter was so concerned about her. Carl had found nothing of any real importance in her flat. All they knew for certain was that her name was Rachel and, judging by the amount of condoms in her bedside drawer and the information in her business diary, she was a careful, expensive prostitute. There was nothing that Dave would consider threatening about her. Carl had been through the contacts in her diary and Peter was not a client, nor were any of his known associates or rivals. She operated without a pimp, so it seemed, which lead Dave to conclude that she was more of a self-employed escort and not a common whore.

What power had she over Peter? That was the question that rattled around in Dave's head and kept his attention away from his eavesdropping. Everything was about power to Peter and Dave knew that. If Peter was scared of someone it was because they had more power than he did. At times, he lowered his paper and leaned forward in an effort to concentrate but he strained to hear the conversation above the hubbub around him. High-spirited banter about the lovely dress and the humorous bets about the suspected length of the marriage where too loud and numerous for him to focus with any efficiency. He heard talk of someone but did not catch a name. He was not so sure that he had gathered enough information to report back to Peter and knew better than to second-guess the missing pieces of a conversation himself. A lesson he had learned before. He knew Peter had a lot to lose and this girl was a threat, if only he could work out why and use the information to his advantage. Dave worked on a principle that knowledge equals power and power could raise the fees for his services. Maybe it could elevate Dave above Peter and give him something to hold over him. He knew Peter would respect that, although not entirely agree with it, or like it.

Dave saw the door move and the narrow gap widened. Rachel stepped out followed by the civil servant that had conducted the meeting. Dave pretended to read the paper as Rachel meandered her way through the chattering wedding guests and then he followed her out moments later. She was pre-occupied; fumbling through her handbag as Dave watched her waiting for the green man at the pelican crossing. She flicked her head back as she finished in her bag and brushed her hand through her long, blonde hair. She raised a pair of sunglasses and slotted them onto her head to keep her hair from slipping forward over her face. A piece of confetti had come to rest on her shoulder and she instantly brushed it off; almost disgusted that the slightest hint of that out-dated institution should make contact with her. Armed with her brother's details on a letterhead from the Registry Office, Rachel took the short walk across the square to the Town Hall. She skipped up the grand stairs between the tall pillars and pushed her way through the revolving doors. A man in a suit greeted her in the reception and soon after ushered her into a small office.

By the time Dave saw her emerge from the Town Hall, Rachel had gathered the last known whereabouts of her brother from the electoral register. Finding a missing sibling had proved an awful lot easier than finding a missing mother. There were fewer hindrances and the paperwork was readily available to any member of the public, relative or no. With her high-heels clicking, she trotted off into the bus station and then stopped to look at a large street map near the entrance. She traced the route along the roads and had to squint to read some of the street names behind the scratched plastic cover. There was a yellow line and a blue one running near the street she needed to find. A quick glance at the key told her she could catch a 16 from Stand B or the 12 from Stand F. Rachel quickly looked at her watch and headed off to Stand F which was the nearest of the two. She scanned the timetable and then quickly skipped across the bus lanes to Stand B. The next bus was due in a few minutes.

Dave had been watching from the edge of the station. He was leaning forward on a railing and smoking a cigarette.

When he saw Rachel settle herself on a long bench at the bus stop, he flicked the cigarette into the road in front of him and started toward the stand for the bus. As he neared the crossing, he felt a firm tap on his shoulder.

"Excuse me, sir?" said a flat, gruff voice behind him.

"Yeah?"

"Littering is an offence, sir and this is a no smoking area," said the man as he flipped open a writing pad, "I'm afraid I'm going to have to give you a ticket,"

"This offence carries a fixed penalty notice, sir," he added as he pointed to a small sign on the railing.

Dave stared for a moment at the man in his red jumper with "Street Warden" written in green on the left breast.

"You what? You having a laugh?"

"No sir! I'll need some details, please sir."

"What?" Dave was astonished. He looked up and saw the number 16 bus crawling to a halt at a set of traffic lights just a junction away from the station.

"I've got to get this bus!" Dave said with a stifled laugh.

"I'm sorry, sir. If you don't give me your name and address for this fixed penalty notice, I will have to have you arrested," the man spoke in a very matter-of-fact tone.

Another man in a similar sweater had appeared and stood shoulder to shoulder with his colleague. Dave was furious with the ridiculous predicament. In his astonishment and anger he shook his head, shrugged his shoulders and raised his hands in disbelief. He became so angry he clenched his fists but he was all too aware of a small group of shoppers waiting for another bus nearby. They had seen what had happened and were watching the whole spectacle with much amusement. Dave could not decide whether to laugh or attack this imbecile that stood before him and threatened him with a fine.

"Sir? Do you have any ID?" the warden insisted.

"OK," Dave surrendered and gave him Carl's name and date of birth. He struggled to remember the house number so he made an educated guess, clinging on to a feint memory of a conversation he had with Carl several weeks ago.

"But I don't have any ID on me to confirm that. Sorry!" Dave shrugged sarcastically.

"No problem, sir, I can check it out," he said as he walked away a couple of paces.

Dave watched as the Warden spoke into his radio. He repeated the details and after a crackle and a click, the Warden returned.

"OK sir, that all checks out."

The warden wrote the ticket and explained about the 'no littering' and 'no smoking' laws as he handed it to Dave. The audience smiled; they seemed suitably entertained by the whole exhibition. The wardens turned to leave and Dave stood shocked into silence. The onlookers eventually drifted their attention to their own conversations. Dave looked down at the ticket.

"£80? Cheeky bastards!" he whispered as he scrunched up the paper and threw it on the floor.

Dave noticed that the lights had changed and the bus was steadily nearing the station. He saw the waiting shoppers get up off the bench and form an orderly queue at the edge of the kerb. He joined them at the back as he kept his eye on Rachel.

After a short, bumpy bus ride, Rachel found herself strolling through a run-down council estate where the roads were numbered rather than named.

"Service Road 12?" she questioned as she walked down a cul-de-sac edged with a row of garages. The roads seemed to meander into dead ends surrounded by streets that crossed each other like a maze. All the houses looked the same, save for the fading paintwork of various colours. The similarities continued into the open-plan gardens, each in various states of maintenance, divided only by Walks, Ways and Groves. Rachel's happiness was slowly eroding away as she traipsed down one long pavement after another, trying to find Campbell Grove. She thought for a moment she had been going round in circles. The whole place was a labyrinth of identical streets and most of the signs had been either damaged or graffitied to the point of illegibility. Eventually, she asked a little girl riding her bicycle if she knew where it was. The girl pointed and shouted without stopping.

Dave was nervous as he followed her. He knew she was lost and thought it would be obvious that he was following her. The streets were open and now and again, from the corner of his eye, he thought he noticed a net curtain in a window twitch. He decided to stay well back and only follow her when she had left his line of sight, which was a risk but he had to stay inconspicuous somehow.

Rachel eventually found the house she was looking for and sighed with relief. It was a run-down end link house, with dirty curtains in the windows and a front door, scratched by impatient dogs over several years, with missing paint and splintered wood. Rachel knocked and waited. She looked across at the window and shivered a little. The curtain moved and a muffled voice shouted from behind the door.

"Wha'd'ya want?"

"I'm looking for James Cooper," she said loudly as she leaned in closer to the door.

"Who are you?"

"His sister."

The door opened slowly and a scruffy young man in a long trench coat stood in front of her. A small black and brown dog ran quickly from behind him, which startled Rachel, and raced across the lawn to relieve itself against a lamppost. The scruffy man looked her up and down with a thoughtful frown as he scratched his arm.

"Come in," he said, "I'll see if he lives here."

Rachel thought it was a strange comment to make until she had seen enough of the interior to conclude that the house was a commune of sorts and most of the residents appeared to be drop-outs and probably transient. She stood in the hallway and had a clear view through to the kitchen at the end and the living room to her left. There was not much natural light coming in through the dirty windows. Candles provided most of the light, flickering hypnotically from empty beer bottles irregularly placed in any space they seemed to fit. There were two young men sat at the bottom of the stairs to her right sharing a suspiciously large cigarette. They leered at Rachel as she entered the hallway. Another man was in the kitchen and stared at her in silence. He stood for a moment, framed in the doorway, and then sidestepped out of sight. Rachel saw two more young men, huddled together, asleep in tattered blankets on the uncarpeted living room floor. An old TV crackled away to itself in the corner of the room. Rachel recognised the smell in the air and then noticed the drug related paraphernalia on the hearth in the room.

"You cool?" said a young woman's voice behind her.

Rachel turned and nodded as a young woman scurried up to her from the living room. She hugged herself and seemed very nervous. She flitted about like a rodent, jerking and shivering.

"Well you're obviously not a copper. Or from the council," she said quickly in a quiet voice.

"I'm looking for my brother," said Rachel in an almost patronising tone.

Rachel looked down at the short girl dressed in grey and green. She looked so fragile.

"Name?"

"James Cooper."

"James…Cooper… …James…? I don't know any James," she shivered.

The girl shouted through to the kitchen in a voice that startled Rachel. This nervous little rodent girl had the bellows of an elephant.

"Anybody know James Cooper?" she hollered.

For a few still moments the house filled with murmurs and whispers, the men on the stairs shuffled and shook their heads. Sound of movement emanated through the ceiling. Rachel looked around at the sudden bustle. The sleepers had woken and the two men on the stairs shuffled up.

"Jack's name was Cooper wasn't it?" shouted a voice from the kitchen, out of Rachel's sight.

"I think it was!" said one of the men on the stairs as he nodded slowly to his seated companion.

"Jack!" stated the voice in the kitchen.

"Jack! Jack! Give it back! You don't want to steal that!" rhymed a voice from the living room.

Again the house filled with murmurs and shuffling wrapped in sinister grey laughter with peering eyes.

"He left here ages ago. Had some bad habits did Jack. He had to go. He was a danger to himself," said the voice from the kitchen, ominously.

Rachel walked nervously through the hall, carefully stepped over the legs of the two men at the foot of the stairs, and stood at the door to the kitchen. The air was so thick with smoke that she coughed to clear her throat. She could feel it in her mouth and nose. She recognised the distinctive smell and taste of cannabis. She stepped into the kitchen in time to witness a young man leaning forward, holding the neck of a bottle with the bottom cut off up to his mouth. His friend had a smouldering piece of cannabis resin between two red-hot knives as the smoke filled the bottle. With a sharp intake of breath, the cloud in the bottle disappeared and the man stood up fast. He breathed in deeply and his eyes widened. Time seemed to stop for moment and everything remained motionless until he exhaled. He handed the bottle to his friend who had returned the two knives to the gas ring on the cooker, cleverly balanced with the ends just inside the flames. Rachel noticed that there were several more small lumps of resin on the worktop next to the cooker.

"You cool?" asked the man as he run his fingers through his long, thick, black hair. He shook his head and slapped his cheeks like a playful chimp.

"Yeah, no worries," Rachel nodded.

"Want a hot-knife?" asked the man by the cooker.

"No thanks," Rachel shook her head, "but don't mind me."

"James was Jack," said the black haired man as he coughed and banged his chest, "you really ought to try that – its good shit!" he added.

"No – not my scene," she shrugged, "He's my brother," she added, "I just want to find out if he's OK."

The black haired man introduced himself as 'Popper'. He offered Rachel a barstool and she sat down. His friend by the cooker took the bottle and Popper held the smouldering knives as he explained about Jack and his problem with thieving.

"No one here likes a thief," he said slowly as he shook his head, "we got next to nothing and what we got we want to keep," he explained.

His friend inhaled the smoke and stood bolt upright, breathing in so deeply that his face turned red. Popper smiled at him and nodded,

"Good stuff innit?"

Popper took the bottle and returned the knives to the hob to redden again. He bobbed up and down like an excited child waiting for something special. He wrung his hands constantly and nodded his head slightly.

"Jack had to go. He took some stuff from a guy called Deck. He's a big fella and not worth crossin'! Heart of gold though, always happy to help, but Jack took the piss. He was cruising for a big one so we smuggled him out before Deck came round enough to kill him. Deck still wants him though, and if he finds him..." his voice trailed off and he shook his head.

"Any idea where he might have gone?" asked Rachel with a sad tone.

Popper inhaled from the bottle and held his breath as he spoke. His chest was fully puffed up and his face reddened. His voice squeaked as he tried desperately to keep the smoke in his lungs for as long as he could,

"He might be with Mickey what's-his-name on Old Station Road. He's a dealer friend of Jack's," Popper shook his head and stifled a laugh which emerged as a wide smile, "right dickhead though! Watch yourself, and don't listen to his bullshit stories!" he added.

Rachel spoke with Popper through several more hotknives until he became too stoned to speak. She became aware that she was more than slightly light-headed herself. Popper became slower and more slurred until he could not string a sentence together at all. When Rachel got up to leave, he could hardly hold his eyes open. She was surprised he could walk her to the door.

"Cheers, Popper. You're a good man. Thanks for your help."

Rachel left the house and realised that she had been passive smoking in the kitchen. The breath of fresh air was startling and the colours all around her seemed a shade or two more vibrant. The sound of happy children playing in the distance and birds singing in nearby trees allowed Rachel to relax. She giggled to herself when she accepted that she was high. At the end of the short walk out to the road, she looked left and right and saw the bus stop that she had got off earlier, not fifty metres from where she stood. She laughed again as she remembered the great trek she had taken to find Popper's place. Dave stood inconspicuously at the end of a nearby alleyway like a private eye tailing an unfaithful wife. He watched her cross the road and vanish behind the houses. He took out his phone and flipped it open.

"Carl? Got a job on mate!"

* * * * *

Rachel stared out of the window of the bus with a slight hint of sadness in her eyes. The effects of the cannabis had sent her into an extraordinarily thoughtful trance and she felt incredibly hungry. She could hear the distant sound of music in her ears and her limbs felt pleasantly heavy and extremely relaxed. As she thought about her brother being involved with drugs, a wave of depression flowed over her and she felt nauseous. She rested her forehead against the cold window and watched the dirty streets fly by. Her mind became a riot of colourful thoughts, dragging her deeper and deeper into herself and further away from the reality outside of her senses.

When she arrived in town she headed straight for a newsagent's shop and bought a multi-pack of crisps that she ate within minutes. Her need for food was unnatural; she was convinced that she had never felt so ravenous in all her life. Floating pleasantly along the street, she found the tail end of a queue at a sandwich bar. She stood for what seemed like far too long staring into the display cabinet, trying to make sense of all the colours and textures she could see humming behind the glass. She giggled to herself, realising that she was still stoned. By the time she had finished eating her snack, she had forgotten what she had bought and the empty crisp packets in her handbag confused her. She decided to walk over to the river and sit on the bank for a while to clear her head. Her search could not go on until she could think straight. She wasted an enlightening couple of hours watching the world go by, solving irrelevant problems and noticing strange aspects of texture and colour that she had never noticed before. The world was a different place when she finally stood up and left the town centre.

Rachel knew Old Station Road was not very far from where she was and so she chose to walk, giving her even more time to balance her mind. As she walked down Chester Street she noticed yellow tape tied around a lamppost and across the path to a fence. It rattled loudly as it fluttered in the breeze. Beside it, a police sign stated 'Serious Incident Here' with a date and a local telephone number. There was a small posy of purple flowers on the ground, leant up against the wall. She walked around the cordoned off area and looked at the large stain on the pavement. It was a very dark red, almost black. Curiously, Rachel stopped and stared. She felt empty headed and nauseous. Her mouth was dry. With a deep breath, she gathered herself together and continued into Old Station Road to look for a house that appeared to belong to a drug dealer. She immediately ruled out the smart houses and made sweeping generalisations about the curtains and furnishings she could see from the street, which helped her narrow down her search. A telephone repairman stopped his tinkering in a green box as Rachel passed. He smiled and nodded. Rachel returned the gesture. He went back to his work while sneaking a peek at Rachel's legs. After a short process of elimination, Rachel had narrowed down three houses on the one side of the street. She stood on the kerb and scanned the opposite row. One house immediately jumped out at her and she dismissed her other prime suspects without a second thought. She looked across the road at the dirty net curtains and faded paint on the front door. It was so obvious that she wondered how she never managed to see it before.

"You must be Mickey!" she whispered.

The repairman looked up from his work again and stared at Rachel without her seeing. He nodded to his colleague in the van parked a short distance away from him. His colleague nodded back. Mickey answered the door in his boxer shorts with his pale, overweight body slumped over the elasticated waistband.

"Who are you?" he mumbled.

"James Cooper? Jack?"

"What?"

"Are you Mickey?"

"Who's asking?"

"I'm looking for Jack," she said flatly.

Mickey stood in silence and stared at Rachel. He scratched himself with his fist in his shorts and leaned forward to look out onto the street. The repairmen across the road had taken a break and were drinking tea in their van. He looked her up and down and whispered,

"You better come in."

Rachel followed Mickey cautiously into the living room. The house made her feel dirty and she wondered about the risk she might be taking.

"What happened?" she quizzed in a sharp tone.

"Who are you? What do you want Jack for?" Mickey sounded nervous as he looked out the window through a narrow gap in his curtains.

"I'm Jack's sister. I need to find him."

Mickey paced the room anxiously and explained that Jack had been attacked in the street. He wiped his forehead and breathed deeply. Rachel questioned the incident and immediately knew it had happened in the taped-off area that she had seen on her way.

"It was serious, that attack you know!" she said, remembering the posy.

85

"Too fuckin' right it was! One of those bastards nicked our gear and now we're in the shit!" Mickey slightly raised his voice and his face reddened.

He took a packet of cigarettes from the mantle and lit one up.

"No. I mean I think someone was seriously hurt, maybe even died! Where's Jack now?"

Mickey did not know what to say. He had not considered the possibility that the attacker may have been injured too. He exhaled a large blue-grey cloud of foul smelling smoke and then offered the packet to Rachel.

"No! Where's Jack?" her voice was stern and firm.

"Hospital. He got hit pretty bad. Stabbed him they did!" Mickey's voice trembled.

Rachel felt almost immune to shocking revelations now but still she felt a tremor of fear shoot through her system and focus on her ribs.

"His blood ... on the path ... was that?" she stuttered as she rubbed her side, curious at the sudden discomfort she felt.

"You're standing in his blood. I thought he was dead!"

Rachel looked down and took a step back. She began to feel a little sick. Mickey offered her a seat and a cup of tea, which were both declined. Mickey was shaking and Rachel could not help but notice that he was sweating a lot despite the cold in the house and him not being dressed.

"He never mentioned anything about a sister!" said Mickey suspiciously.

"He doesn't know he has one yet!" Rachel stated with a wry smile.

* * * * *

Carl had Popper by the throat and held him up against the wall. His friend was unconscious on the kitchen floor. The rodent girl was leaning up against the doorframe pinching her bleeding nose. Two other men were barely conscious on the floor in the hall nursing painful torsos and bruised faces. They groaned quietly to themselves as they tried to crawl away towards the door.

"What did she want?" growled Dave from behind Carl.

"You pussy! You can't even do your own dirty work!" Popper struggled to get loose of the tight grip on his neck.

Carl threw Popper across the room and he landed in a heap on the floor with a groan.

"How many times have we got to do this?" said Dave as Carl picked Popper up by the neck again and thrust him against the wall.

"Fuck you!" Popper spat blood in Carl's face.

Carl threw Popper again and he slid along a worktop before crashing into the sink and rolling onto the floor. The rodent girl was standing in the doorway, seemingly unmoved by the brutal display of violence. She turned around quickly when she heard the front door open. A large man came in and instantly appeared to fill the hallway; the room had become noticeably darker. He was a hulk of a man, standing broad and tall with full sleeve tattoos down each arm. A black moustache underlined a gold ring through the centre of his nose. A Mauri styled tattoo wrapped around his left eye, across the side of his head and around his ear. His head was shaved, save for a single, long, plait at the back, tied with a bright red band.

"Thank fuck you're here, Deck!" said the girl, "These twats are kicking off!"

Deck strode past the rodent girl in the doorway and stood in the kitchen facing Carl who had hold of Popper again. He towered over him and Carl stared up in disbelief.

"Put him the fuck down!" growled Deck slowly, as he pressed his hand around Carl's throat.

Carl felt the pressure in his temples build up immediately and knew his face must have been turning purple. He let go of Popper and Dave took a step back. Deck had Carl at arm's length in front of him and raised him slowly up in the air. Carl's feet hovered uselessly a few inches off the floor. His heartbeat pounded in his head. He thought for a moment his eardrums would bleed if he did not lose consciousness first. Popper struggled to his feet and wiped the blood from his chin. Dave stood staring in disbelief, pulled at his collar and cufflinks and walked towards the back door. He pulled it wide and walked nervously down the garden path, with an ever-increasing gait. Deck threw Carl out of the open doorway and into the garden where he fell in a heap on the overgrown lawn. The intimidating giant strode over to the door and stood with his arms crossed. He had to stoop and pull his arms in to fit within the frame. Carl struggled to find his bearings and had to sit a moment or two to catch his breath. Momentarily, his face paled back to normal and the pounding in his ears diminished. Deck raised two fingers to his eyes and turned them to point at Carl.

"If I see you again," he threatened, "you're dead!"

Carl struggled to his feet and brushed himself down. He stood and stared at Deck for a moment before he turned to leave the garden. Dave had gone.

Chapter 5

Jack had discharged himself from the hospital as soon as he was able, albeit against the best advice of the nurses on the ward and the doctor doing the rounds. He was not feeling as fit as he would have liked but at least he had eaten something and managed to get a wash. The doctor had assured him it was a 'lucky' wound and told him the age-old 'another inch to the left' anecdote. Jack did not consider it so lucky, even though it did only just miss his lung. He had numerous stitches that stung as he strolled aimlessly down a street lined with shops, meandering through the people at his own pace. They stared back at him as they always did, with judging eyes and disagreeable frowns. He feared Kit would be out to find him, probably want to beat him or possibly even kill him. He suspected that the police had Mickey's house under surveillance so he stayed clear of that part of town, however tempting the sanctuary appeared to be. Suddenly, he remembered the address of the boy that had stolen his gear.

Leaning on a lamppost to catch his breath, he caught the irresistible smell of fish and chips wafting from a café that had the front door open. The diners looked so content and the café welcoming. He limped his way over to the nearest table by the door and ordered a plate of haddock, chips and peas, a cup of tea and some bread and butter. After a few long minutes a young waitress put his food in front of him with a polite smile. Jack resisted the urge to scoff the food down and deliberately took his time. He savoured the tea. The drinks in the hospital had tasted like the plastic cups they came in and he had not had a decent brew for days. When the other diners were engrossed in their meals and private conversations, he quietly asked the waitress for the bill. She went behind the till at the far end of the shop and as she turned her back to Jack, he got up and slipped out as quickly as his painful wound would allow.

He walked swiftly with a slight limp, and eventually started to jog with a little hop. His stitches were hot and began to sting so he pressed his hand against them as he groaned. Suddenly, an annoyed female voice filled the street and attracted the attention of all within earshot. The waitress stood on the pavement outside the café door, scowling with her middle finger raised in his direction.

Grimacing through the ever-increasing burning sensation in his ribs, he picked up his pace a little and ran into a side street. He did not know why he was running. The waitress had not followed him but the urge to run kept him moving for a while, as if he could escape his situation and leave his life behind. Optimistic thoughts echoed the encouragement he needed to block out the pain. Unfortunately, the fish and chips had not settled in his stomach and he felt the onset of cramp, alongside a steadily growing dizziness as his heart rate increased. He rounded a corner into a small shopping area on the outskirts of the town centre and dashed out across the road with his head down watching his feet. His dizziness grew and he slowed down a little. As he raised his face to see where he was going, he bumped into a woman and knocked her to the floor. He stumbled and landed on top of her.

The nearby shoppers scattered like a flock of startled pigeons, evading an immediate danger. Jack stared into her green eyes with amazement. Her long, blonde hair splayed out on the pavement like an awesome, fiery halo. She was beautiful, like an actress in a hair product commercial. Ensnared by her splendour, he stared for a timeless moment, then suddenly noticed her handbag had slipped from her grasp and landed just out of reach. He instinctively grabbed it as he got to his feet and ran off down the street with newfound stamina. Rachel got up and screamed after him. Several shoppers stopped what they were doing to look, but not one of them reacted to her cry for help. Jack left the coolness of the shadow and entered the warmer light of the autumn sun as he crossed the street. Looking back to where the woman was standing, still shouting, he smiled at his victory. Suddenly, as he turned to see where he was going, he felt the full force of a fist hit him between the eyes. The impact lifted him off his feet and threw him half on to the pavement and half in the road as he slumped down at the foot of a lamppost. Startled shoppers gasped in shock as they became still for a moment and stared. Carl had been following

Rachel and had seen the whole thing. He stared down at Jack, unconscious on the floor, and nodded slowly as he rubbed his hands together.

Rachel started to run across the street to where Jack lay. Carl saw her coming and slipped into the flow of people before he ducked into a doorway out of sight. A small crowd had gathered although most people just wanted to get by without getting involved in the aggression. Rachel stood over Jack as she snatched back her handbag and looked around for her saviour. He was nowhere to be seen, and she was not entirely sure she would have recognised him anyway. She heard Jack murmuring and shuffling as he was coming round so she turned to leave before he became fully aware of what was happening. His nose throbbed as he struggled to his feet, but there was no blood, which surprised him. Rachel watched him staggering about in the gutter as she walked quickly out of sight. Carl was standing in a shop doorway and relaying the live commentary into his mobile phone.

* * * * *

High up in Peter's office, Dave sat back in a swivel chair as he returned his phone to his inside pocket. He explained the events described to him over the phone. He told Peter about Rachel and her lifestyle, about visits to the Registry Office, and how he suspected she was looking for someone but he did not know whom. He explained about the house on the estate.

"Rachel?" Peter mused, "she could be anybody!" he whispered, "Did the hippies tell you anything?" he added sharply.

"We didn't get shit from them. We had a spot of bother," stuttered Dave, hoping there would be no questions.

"Bother? What the hell do I pay you for?" Peter shook his head and walked around the table. He stood and looked out of the office window across the skyline,

"This Rachel? Where did Carl say she was going when she got attacked?"

"She was following up a lead on who she's looking for. I don't think its you. I think it's someone else. I don't think she has anything to do with you!"

"Well it's a good job I don't pay you to think then, isn't it?" replied Peter as he paced the room.

"She has found a Sally Cooper though. On the Manor Garth estate," added Dave.

Peter's face dropped and he stopped in his tracks. He instantly felt sick and cold. He turned to face Dave.

"Who?" he stuttered with wide eyes.

"Sally Cooper. Ring a bell?" asked Dave, although he knew that it obviously did.

Peter looked at the floor and rubbed his hands together. His mind's eye instantly replayed the night in the Hotel and the photograph in the purse. Shocking revelations sparked in his thoughts. He paced nervously until he sat opposite Dave. His face was pale and he was shaking slightly. Dave could see his hands trembling as they rested in front of him on the table.

"I thought she was dead! How did she find her?" he whispered to himself.

Dave leaned forward and tried to look Peter in the eye but his gaze was darting about the room and impossible to lock onto. Peter stood up and paced again. He swore under his breath. Dave looked on; Peter was really worried about Sally Cooper, whoever she was. He was more concerned about her than Rachel. This was a card Dave could play close to his chest. There was potential here, if only Dave could unlock it.

"OK," Peter said calmly as he took a seat at the head of the table, "here's the plan. Get the hippies to talk. Follow that up as soon as you know something. You keep your fuckin' mind on the job and find out who she's looking for!" his voice raised in proportion with his rising anger as he spoke.

Dave stood up, tugged his cufflinks and pulled his collar as he turned to the door. Peter remained seated with his hands nervously tapping the table.

"And silence Sally Cooper," he added without emotion.

* * * * *

92

Jack was annoyed and cursing himself under his breath. Not only did his ribs hurt but now his nose was throbbing too. Why did he have to steal everything? Why did he have to get himself into so much trouble? He knew thieving was wrong, but only ever in hindsight. He could never reason with his own conscience at the times when it mattered. He never even considered leaving the bag alone; the thought simply did not enter his mind. He walked through the shopping centre to a large paved area with an ornamental fountain in the centre and benches around the outside. A couple of elderly drunks fed the pigeons and a young girl played with sticks on a grassed area while her parents watched from a nearby bench. Jack took a seat where the sun could warm him. He leaned forward and pulled up his socks beneath his jeans, tightened his boots and straightened out the layers of clothes in an attempt to find some comfort. The parents of the playful girl were looking over suspiciously and talking to each other while pointing at Jack. It was nothing new to him; lots of people pointed and stared. He took a cigarette out of a packet from his pocket and lit it up. He drew hard on the filter but nothing much came through. Puzzled, he looked at the cigarette.

"Shit!" he whispered.

There was a slight tear in the paper near the filter. He rummaged in his pocket to find his cigarette papers and began to cover the damage. He had just finished when he noticed Kit walking towards him from the grassed area.

"Shit!" he said in a slightly louder whisper.

He did not think she had noticed him yet but it was just a matter of time. What could he do? If he stayed put, she would see him and come over. At least if that were the case he could get it over with now. She was alone and it was broad daylight, so it would not be such a bad beating. If he ran away, she would see him running and maybe give chase. She might be able to catch him with his wound slowing him down, but how fast was she in those big heavy boots? Jack pondered the possibilities as he watched Kit getting ever closer. Jack tried to reason in his mind but his paranoia and fear took over as he slowly got to his feet. He turned with the intention of running away from the busy shopping area, but as he raised his eyes to check his escape route, he saw Jonny walking slowly towards him.

"Shit!"

He looked back at Kit and she waved to him with a big sarcastic smile. From the corner of his eye he saw Jonny wave also. He turned to run in the opposite direction and saw another large man walking towards him, also waving.

"Shit! Shit! Shit!"

Jack looked at the three of them advancing menacingly then scanned the other people ambling through the streets and across the grass. He took what he assumed to be the lesser of the risks as he ran as fast as he could towards Kit with the intention of dodging around her. She stopped in her tracks, leaned forward slightly and waited for him with her arms out to her side, as if paused in an appreciative bow at the end of a Shakespearean tragedy. As he neared her, he noticed a shiny object in her hand as it caught a glimmer of sunshine and immediately knew she had a knife. He veered off to the right and ran around the unknown man into the streets beyond. His ribs were screaming in pain but he was too scared to let it register. The unknown man turned to run but fortunately for Jack, he was slow and clumsy on his feet. He almost stomped headlong into a young couple with a baby and had to jump aside to avoid knocking over the pram. Jonny had begun to run but he was too slow in getting to the street. By the time he had rounded the corner, Jack was safely out of sight.

Jack ran as he had never run before; hot feet pounded against the pavement as his throat became cold and painful. His ribs were stinging and he suspected that his stitches had come loose. Continuing through the town centre, weaving through the throng of shoppers, he hurtled towards the bus station. He jumped over a railing with a single handed vault and landed with a sudden jolt that took the wind out of him. A couple of quick deep breaths later, he jogged into a pub. He bumped himself lazily into a wall and flopped down onto a wooden chair. With aching legs rested out in front of him and limp arms hung loosely by his sides, he panted heavily and stared at the ceiling as he gathered his thoughts and his breath.

"Trouble, son?" asked a friendly female voice from behind the bar.

Too breathless to speak Jack just raised a thumb in the general direction of the barmaid and nodded. He reached under his jumper to his wounded ribs and gave them a gentle stroke. He pulled his hand away and checked for blood. There was none. Still convinced he must have been bleeding and that something was wrong, he got up slowly and went through to the Gents. He locked himself in a cubicle and put the lid down on the toilet before he took off his coat and hung it on the back of the door. Stripped down to his bare chest, he checked his stitches, which were red but not bleeding. They hurt like hell. Jack stared and toyed with the wound. With morbid fascination, he watched the flesh pull up into tiny peaks as he tugged at the stitching. Temptation dared him to pull harder and although he knew he would not do it, the slight onset of pain was quite pleasurable.

The pub was almost empty save for a couple of old grey sea dogs that sat staring into empty glasses with nothing to say to each other. Only the barmaid seemed to be alive as she floated from one lifeless table to another collecting glasses. Jack walked slowly around the tables and helped himself to the dregs from three remaining glasses. Just in case his chasers had followed him, he peered out of the door before he stepped out to the street. His pain and discomfort had been increasing and now he needed to rest; somewhere he could stay without getting paranoid, somewhere he did not have to look over his shoulder all the time. He scanned the street and saw 'The Haven'; a resting-place for the homeless that offered warm food and temporary shelter. The staff knew Jack and he had friends of a sort that frequented the place. He took a deep breath and headed out toward the main entrance, his mind full of warm thoughts and welcoming memories.

* * * * *

Rachel tried to get some information about Jack from a nurse who, like a tight-lipped oyster sealed shut to guard a precious pearl, was stubbornly sticking to her patient confidentiality rule. She would not inform Rachel where he had gone after he signed himself out, even though she had the letterhead from the Registry Office and another from the Town Hall, proving her relationship to him. Rachel became angry and feared that the trail was in danger of growing cold. The nurse held fast from behind her desk. She was very apologetic and insisted that she understood, which made Rachel even angrier. Cautiously, and successfully concealing her growing annoyance, she continued the questioning in an attempt to chip away at the hard outer casing to get at her prize. When she saw that the direct approach was not working, she tried a different tack. She explained almost tearfully how she was tracking down her long-lost brother that she never knew she had, emphasising the sadness of the torn family to gain sympathy. Rachel was at last wearing down the nurse and her shell was beginning to crack.

"Let me speak to the Ward Manager," nodded the nurse supportively as she picked up a phone.

Rachel took a seat for a few minutes until a grey-haired man in a suit and half-moon spectacles came out to greet her. He had a cardboard wallet under his arm, hugged to his chest. They went into a small office and Rachel handed him the letters from the Local Authority. They sat opposite each other at a square desk.

"Hmmm, you really are having an exciting time, aren't you?"

For a few moments he stared down at the letters and hummed. He scanned them interestingly and nodded here and there. Rachel wondered what on earth could have attracted his attention, as there were no fine details or small print. They were just ordinary letters, read and understood instantly, but this academic certainly made a meal of them. When he reached the end, he straightened the papers on his desk and looked at Rachel patronisingly from over the top of his spectacles. Rachel could feel herself becoming angry again after she had tried so hard to calm down.

"I just want to know where my brother is," she said slowly in an effort to restrain her frustration.

"I can offer some information to help you in your search, which I think may not be confidential under these very special circumstances," he began as he removed his spectacles.

He opened the cardboard file and ran his finger across the edge of the papers to align them all together. Again, his gaze wandered all over the page, as if he was reading in a random order rather than the more customary left to right. He hummed and nodded as he went.

"His records say that he is NFA – that's 'no fixed abode'. He doesn't live anywhere, he's homeless."

Rachel shook her head discreetly and felt as if she needed to scream very loud.

"The only contact address he has given in case of an emergency is a place called 'The Haven' on Queen Elizabeth Road, by the shopping precinct. We work with them a lot," he sounded very proud.

"When you get there, ask for Dr Rudkin or Dr Crowe. Either of those good people will know me and help you," he pointed at himself and then at Rachel with his spectacles before he popped them back on.

He looked at her from above the rims again and waited there with his hands clasped in front of him on the desk as he circled his thumbs irritatingly. Rachel stared at him; wishing that he could sense the expletives she was thinking to tell him how rude and patronising he was.

* * * * *

Jack entered the reception area of The Haven and immediately felt relaxed. He was safe here, he was sure. He felt confident that Kit would not find him here and even if she did, CCTV covered the whole place so she would not try anything. Jack booked himself in and accepted the offer of a three-night stay. He took a room upstairs on the first floor. It was a box-room, with a bed, a small cabinet and a small en-suite shower and toilet. The window overlooked the pub he had crashed in earlier and he could see all the way down the busy high street. He took advantage of the shower and the communal laundry room down the hall. By teatime he felt fresh, relaxed and clean. He breezed into the dining room and took a seat near enough to a window to see out yet close enough to the wall so he could hide if necessary. He looked around the room at the bedraggled souls hunched over their own tables, wrapped in shrouds of misery and depression. Jack thought it was relatively empty, considering the recent cold nights. A hunched up old man, cowering behind his stubble and grey hair yellowing with dirt, reminded Jack of an old friend; the man that had taught him about 'warm spots' when he had first hit the streets. He advised Jack to look for air-vents and other outlets from buildings where the warm air from the central heating systems belched out into the cold night.

"The fumes and the heat will help you sleep!" he used to laugh in his grey, gruff voice.

He gave Jack many tips to survive being homeless, some of them useful; others were just too risky. Like the tale he told of how he stepped out into oncoming traffic in a deliberate attempt to hospitalise himself. He had done it every winter to get a warm bed and well fed over the Christmas season and if he died in the attempt, who would miss him? What did he have to lose? He died two winters ago, beneath the wheels of a family car. Jack missed his company and he had no doubt that the family in the car would never forget him either, even though they only ever met him once.

Jack had never thought that seriously about his own pointlessness and somewhere deep inside, hoped for another way out of this hell he had created for himself. He had hope, and he clung on to it for dear life. One of these days he would find his redemption. He pulled his coat sleeves down over his hands and inhaled the fresh fragrance of the washing detergent as he waited for his afternoon meal. It reminded him that there was still goodness out there somewhere. He still had a chance to get back to the reality he had lost so long ago. Just as his meal arrived, he saw a familiar face walking towards him with the woman from reception next to her, gesturing towards Jack.

"Shit!" he whispered as he stood up quick.

"It's OK," said Rachel as she approached, "I just need to speak with you."

She sat opposite Jack and looked up at him with her green eyes. Jack fidgeted and felt uncomfortable. He was confused. He tried to work out what was going on but the logic eluded him. The woman from reception, sensing Jack's discomfort, stayed a short distance away, not really sure what to do. She looked at Jack and nodded questioningly with her eyebrows raised. Jack nodded back. She waved her hand and returned to the reception desk.

"Please sit with me?" asked Rachel.

A humble and sorry Jack sat down and pulled his bowl closer to him as if he was guarding it from her. He tore his bread roll to pieces and dropped some chunks into the soup. He did not look up at her, even though the temptation to lose himself in her beautiful green eyes was beckoning him, his sense of guilt and shame dropped his gaze to his meal.

"My name is Rachel Masters. You're James Cooper."

"Just Jack," he replied defensively between slurps of soup.

"Why? Why change your name?"

"None of your business, is it? I suppose you got your bag back?"

Rachel suddenly realised she was talking to the same man that had bumped into her in the street, but she had not recognised him. He looked different with his clean hair combed and his chin shaved of stubble, but now that he had mentioned it, she recognised him easily and wondered why she did not make the connection sooner.

"That's OK. Don't worry about that," she said reassuringly, "I have news for you, Jack."

Rachel took the photograph from her purse and put it on the table in front of him. He stared down at it as he wiped the sides of his bowl with his remaining chunks of bread.

"Yeah? And?" he quizzed aggressively.

"It's you!" said Rachel, "That's you and your mother. For years ... well ... all my life actually, I thought it was me, but apparently … it's you," her voice wavered slightly and she felt as if she would cry.

"Me?" he muffled with his mouth full, "What you got it for then?"

"I'm your sister, Jack! Your twin sister!" Rachel whispered.

Somewhere in the back of his mind a light switched on and showed him the escape route he had been looking for. Could this woman be his salvation? He looked up at her for the first time since she had sat down. She certainly appeared angelic with her blonde halo hair and beautiful green eyes. Jack stared at the photograph, then at Rachel, then back at the photograph again. The pair sat in silence for an uncomfortable moment before they both tried to speak at the same time. Jack excused himself and allowed Rachel to continue,

"I've been looking for my mother for years now and then I found out that I had a brother too."

Rachel told him her date of birth, which was, as expected, the same as Jack's. She explained about the successful search for her mother and the state of her house. She told him, however briefly, the story of their father and the reasons for their separation. She joked about it being he that made her ill in the womb and her eyes were a constant reminder of her lack of nutrition in her foetal stage. Jack sat in silence, listening without comment until Rachel had explained the whole story.

Jack was busy plotting in his mind. What if she was mistaken and this was all a coincidence? What could it mean if this was all true? What did he have to lose? He could not remember enough of his broken childhood to dispute or confirm anything of what she said. Adolescence fuelled with cannabis and hallucinogens had all but erased his childhood memories and the fragments he could recall were more than a little hazy. As they stumbled their way through their splintered conversation, a tall woman with a name badge on a chain around her neck approached the table,

"Would you like desert, Jack? Would your friend like some too? It's hot apple pie and custard," she interrupted with a soft voice.

"Yes ... please ... for us both," stuttered Jack, looking up at the woman, hoping that Rachel would refuse hers and he could have two servings.

Rachel waited for a further response from Jack but none came. She leaned forward, expecting something but he was blank.

"Well?" she questioned.

"Well ... wow!" he said, "It's a bit much to take in right now!"

Rachel tried hard to keep the fractured conversation together and make friends with Jack. She felt more than slightly awkward and Jack's own discomfort never made things any easier for the pair of them. Jack eventually apologised for stealing the handbag and explained about his thieving being almost instinctual. He was quite open about his habit and the need to steal to fuel his cravings.

"I spoke to Popper," she warned, "Deck is still after you!"

"Oh shit! That's all I need!" he shrugged, "I thought he would have forgotten about that by now!"

He pushed his bowl towards the centre of the table and sat back in his chair with satisfied warmth in his stomach.

"What did you take?"

"It was nothing really, just a locket. I sold it for some gear."

"Did you not think it might be worth something to him? A keepsake or something sentimental?"

"I didn't think Deck was like that, did I? Have you seen him? He's not the kind of bloke to give a shit really. I didn't expect him to go soft about some stupid locket! I mean, it's not like it had a photo in it or anything!"

Rachel shook her head in disbelief. Jack had started to shiver a little.

"You OK?"

"Just hanging out a bit, that's all. It's under control, though," he added defensively, "just some days are worse than others. I got a little bit of my own gear left and I can get Meth here, that'll help."

After a short, apprehensive silence, Jack got up and went out to the reception. He was only gone a few short minutes before he returned.

"OK?" enquired Rachel.

"Doctor's going to help me out later tonight, before lights out."

Rachel was at a loss as to what to do. She wanted to get to know Jack but he was overly defensive. Topics of conversation entered her mind and she thought about speaking, but she was hesitant and striking up another conversation was proving difficult. Reluctantly, as a desperate measure, she offered to take Jack into the shopping centre and after a long period of persuasion, he unenthusiastically agreed. She thought it might be an idea to walk and talk, to get to know each other more. All Jack could think about were the people that might be out there looking for him. He thought about the crowds in the precinct, staring at him. The thought of venturing out played on his mind, but the temptation in those beautiful green eyes was too much to resist. The two of them wandered through the precinct just as the last of the shoppers were finishing off. Rachel looked at her watch. It was twenty-five to five.

"I'm sorry Jack. I didn't realise it was getting on."

The two of them became comfortable in each other's company quite quickly, they talked about anything and everything as they focussed on shopping rather than on each other. As Rachel had hoped, the retail therapy had become a pleasant and positive distraction and Jack began to open up a little. They were rapidly becoming friends, much to Jack's surprise as he did not often allow people to get so close, nor did he like to get close to other people. He was a little taken aback when Rachel hooked her arm through his, seemingly without a thought or hesitation, but he smiled and allowed her to hang on to him. He felt proud for a moment and almost forgot about his itching need for a fix. He felt as if he walked taller with her there on his arm, with his chest out and chin up. The concept of having a twin sister was growing on him. Rachel felt confident that Jack would not object to her clinging on to him. She was a little nervous at first and was not sure how to act in a platonic relationship with a man, let alone a brother-sister relationship. All of her previous relationships had been based on sex-for-gain and now she had found her brother she was a little confused as to how to behave. There was no financial benefit for Rachel, only affection; an emotion she had lived without for so long.

They managed to get a good look in one of the smaller department stores where Rachel had found a selection of three-for-two jumpers that she thought Jack might like. He felt awkward about accepting them as a gift but then thought it would be better than stealing them, which he was very tempted to do. He tried one on for size and when he was satisfied with the fit he picked three in different colours. As they left the shopping precinct, Jack noticed Kit, Jonny and the third man walking ahead of them, with their back to him. He shuddered. Rachel noticed, stopped, and looked him in the eye,

"What's up?"

"It's nothing," he lied, "just got a bit of a cold chill that's all."

Jonny turned to enter The Haven as the other two waited by the door. They looked around the street and then in the direction of Jack and Rachel. Jack ducked into a doorway quickly.

"What's going on Jack?" she questioned, slightly angry that he was keeping something important from her.

"Is there somewhere else we can go?" shivered Jack with an obvious hint of fear in his voice.

"Come on," she offered, "We'll go…" she paused. She was going to say 'home' but then changed her mind, "…find a hotel for the night. There's one at the end of the precinct, near Maine Square. I have friends there."

The two walked off, without linking arms, as Jack explained about Kit and her violent friends. He explained that he had enemies now and his life was in serious danger. At first he was reluctant to share these thoughts with her but eventually surrendered. Now Rachel was involved with him, she would also be involved in the threats made against him, and as such, she may be in danger herself. He surmised to himself that if he wanted full redemption, it would cost him his honesty. He should share almost everything with her if she was going to be his escape back to normality. Jack spoke as if he had never spoken before, pouring out everything that was happening in his life. Some statements stumbled out of his mouth before he realised what he was disclosing and he came dangerously close to revealing more than was comfortable. Rachel listened attentively. She had listened to men pour it all out before and this was no different as far as she was concerned, other than her emotional attachment to Jack. She valued the sharing and asked incisive questions, which is something she would never have considered with her clients.

Rachel took out a credit card from her purse and placed it on the desk in front of the receptionist. As if held in the magic spell of the shiny golden plastic, the receptionist smiled a little more brightly and made an extra effort to accommodate the pair with the best room they had available. They were escorted across the finely decorated foyer to the elevator, and then along a brightly lit corridor to a plush apartment style room, with two separate sleeping areas and a large Jacuzzi style bathtub. In the centre of the wide living space sat a broad sofa with thick cushions. Rachel plonked herself down and the soft cushions absorbed her into their comfort.

"I have a confession," started Rachel, "I haven't been entirely open with you."

"Oh shit! What is it?" said Jack, with a hint of anticipated disappointment in his voice.

He fully expected his world to come crashing down again and his salvation to sail off into the distance and drown over the horizon.

"It's ... well ... I'm ... a professional escort," she stuttered, "a prostitute, if you like..." she added after an awkward silence.

There was a long pause while the siblings remained motionless, trapped in thought.

"Oh!" is all he replied.

Rachel sat and stared at the floor, expecting to hear something else. She braced herself, waiting for the onslaught of disapproval or the accusations she had always expected to receive at this point in previous conversations. Jack fidgeted awkwardly and looked about the room. He thought about the statement, something he was not accustomed to doing, and considered his own lifestyle and the things he assumed to be 'normal'. In a rare moment of compassion that Jack found surprisingly comfortable, he turned to Rachel.

"Do you want a cup of tea?" Jack offered, in the firm belief that a good cup of tea would solve almost anything.

Rachel looked up, startled. Her whole body relaxed again. She smiled gently. Jack smiled back. Within that instant of a shared, non-verbal agreement, they sealed a mutual trust.

"Yes, please."

Chapter 6

Peter read the letter several times with a private smile that locked away the dishonest truth behind his deceitful victory. He had neither the time nor the inclination to respond to the quiet voice of guilt that echoed almost silently from his subconscious like a small child trapped in a Dickensian orphanage. Comfortably naked, he walked through his kitchen and dropped the page onto the worktop as he crossed the cold tiled floor to his percolator. He poured a cup of coffee and retrieved the letter on his way back to the living room. As he paused to sip his drink he read it again. It was confirmation of his successful application for funding, exactly as he expected. He had entered a bid for £780,000 towards his Newbury Hall project, which offered rehabilitation to drug addicts and alcoholics alongside life skills training and personal development. The intention was to offer a new start for all those that wanted to escape the self-destructive world of addiction. The local statistics for drug use and drug related crime were on the increase. The number of young people leaving school with no qualifications and little hope of finding employment was also increasing. This gave Peter both an established current and potential supply of clients for years to come. His predatory attitude had helped him realise the benefits of hooking into such a lucrative market and like a hungry leach on an unsuspecting carp, he expected to bleed it for everything he could. The government had increased initiatives to drug related work and lowering crime was always high on their agenda. Peter's plans ticked all the boxes. Acquiring the funding was as honest and easy as picking apples in autumn; the creative accounting to filter off some of the money into his own private overseas account, however, may prove more of a challenge.

He took his coffee and the letter into a small study and booted up his computer. He pulled two lever-arch files and a ream of paper from the back shelf as the ageing operating system chugged slowly through its start up routine. With an annoying beep and a pleasant jingle, the computer indicated that it was ready. Peter squinted at the screen and rolled the mouse back and forth several times before he started replying to or deleting his emails accordingly. When he had filtered through the penis enlargement, free mortgage and 'you've won a prize' junk mails he began to construct his own good news message. He made reference to the funding confirmation letter and quoted paragraphs to his esteemed colleagues in his address book. He bold typed '£780,000' with pride.

He decided he would hold a celebration dinner and dance in the Masonic Lodge to celebrate his success and telephoned his office to have the necessary arrangements made. He read the letter over the phone to his PA, who listened patiently. She humoured him with positive comments and compliments and then informed him she would mail the details, using only the finest quality paper, to all the invited guests for the weekend celebration. When she hung up, she flicked two fingers up to the phone before she returned to her work.

* * * * *

Rachel looked on as Sally and Jack stood together in a hug for what she thought was far too long. She actually felt something that she assumed to be sibling rivalry; an emotion she was not proud to feel but she was pleased to be able to feel something for her reunited family. She jealously wondered how long this hug would last and how much emotion it carried. When Sally pulled away, happy tears had trickled down her cheeks and followed the contours of her wrinkles as they curved around her smile. Holding onto Jack's shoulders, she looked him in the eyes without speaking before she pulled herself into his chest again and whispered something inaudible. She felt so relieved to have her son back with her after all these years. Jack was uncomfortable with being physically touched and tried to keep his distance without actually appearing to be keeping his distance. He hugged half-heartedly and felt slightly repulsed by this strange old woman that until a few moments ago, he did not know. Her hair smelled, and even to a homeless drug addict, it smelled foul. He stood and waited for the emotional display to pass, in an effort to please his sister, but somehow, he knew that this woman needed this moment and he should give it to her. Even though it unsettled him, he allowed her the pleasure.

He had no recollection of his mother and felt nothing towards her. To him, she was a smelly alcoholic, aged beyond her years, who dare not leave the safety of her own home. Jack sat on the couch next to Rachel, hoping he could hide behind his sister or at least use her as a barrier to distance himself from the slightly disturbing woman. Rachel looked at him and smiled as she rested her hand on his knee. He smiled back sheepishly. Sally staggered into her chair and lit herself a cigarette. She tossed one over to Jack and another to Rachel.

"I don't smoke," said Rachel, picking the cigarette up from her lap, feeling sure that she had already shared that conversation with her mother.

"I'll have yours then, I'll save it for 'ron!" smiled Jack as he snatched it from her fingertips and popped it behind his ear.

Sally smiled and threw him a lighter.

"So, James? What do you do now love?" she rasped from her smoke filled lungs.

"It's Jack, not James," he stated flatly, only faintly displaying his true hatred of that name, "I don't do much really. Just make a living any way I can. Bit of this, bit of that, you know?" he looked at the floor and sucked hard on the cigarette.

"When you were a little 'un, you wanted to ride horses!" she cackled, "You used to ride on the carpet sweeper screaming 'yee-har' all around the kitchen!"

"Yeah? I don't know. Can't remember," Jack blew smoke rings down towards the floor.

Sally reminisced with humorous anecdotes about Jack as he watched the smoke rings roll down to the carpet and dissipate like ripples on a pond. He was deliberately distant and only reluctantly commented without any intention of entering into further conversation. He cleverly interjected quick comments in order to redirect the conversation to save him from revealing anything about his life. He was as comfortable with Sally as he had been with Rachel at first. Sally was so happy to have her son with her that she did not notice he was lost in nervous thoughts and paid her no attention. The fractured conversation stumbled, and Rachel, aware of the growing discord, felt uncomfortable. Sally seemed unconditionally attached to Jack and wanted to know everything about him. Rachel felt a little bit jealous of the attention he willingly rejected. After all, it was she that had found her and brought her precious Jack back into the family. It was she that had begun to support her mother out of her alcoholic slump and cleaned her house. Why did she not pay Rachel that much attention?

Rachel thought it was a waste of good affection as Sally showered her interest on Jack and he did nothing to appreciate it. She wanted some of that attention but knew better than to interrupt with some obviously desperate comment to try and steal the limelight. She smiled at Sally and tried to make eye contact but her subtle interjections were unnoticed and her heart sank momentarily. Retreating to the kitchen, which she had spent several hours cleaning, Rachel prepared some sandwiches for everyone. She could hear the conversations that Sally was desperately trying to engage in with Jack and remembered the less enthusiastic reception she had received from her mother when they first met.

"Maybe its because she knew Jack longer when he was a baby," she thought in a whisper, trying to calm herself, "maybe that's it. Maybe she did not know me at all."

She was surprised that her mother had managed to keep the kitchen so clean and barely noticed the new tea stains on the worktop near the kettle. The half-bottle of whiskey in the cupboard did not escape her attention, but she understood that to quit would take her mother a long time. With cups of steaming drinks, she returned to the living room. She set the tray down on a small coffee table and everybody tucked in, like starlings at a bread covered bird table in winter. They sat in a silence broken only by the feint sounds of chewing and drinking. Jack was the first to finish and flopped back onto the couch after he had placed his empty plate back on the coffee table. Casually, he looked about the room at the pictures and the ornaments. A pretty silver clock on the mantle caught his attention, beside a small-framed picture that he could not make out. He got up to take a closer look.

"That's you, son," said Sally between mouthfuls, "straight after you were born."

Rachel was offended; there were no pictures her anywhere. Jack was unmoved. The scratched glass and tarnished frame had faded over time. Jack was looking at a picture of a baby on a mustard-yellow towel. It had its eyes scrunched up tight and mouth wide open as if in the middle of a long, loud scream.

"You were a noisy bugger!" she laughed, spitting crumbs into her lap.

Jack replaced the picture slowly and took a long look at the clock. He guessed it was real silver. The stones looked familiar, probably topaz but he could not be sure. He raised his index finger and slid it across the ornate frame before gently stroking the glass face.

"No, Jack!" said Rachel, in a firm voice.

"Sorry!" he jolted.

With a shrug and a guilty, although apologetic, smile at Rachel, he took his seat, trying to laugh it off in a very guarded, secret joke, kind of way.

"What?" Sally questioned.

Jack looked over at Sally who was staring at him with a big smile. He feared she might pinch his cheeks or kiss him, like an elderly relative at a family get-together. He asked about his father in order to change the subject. The question fell like a judge's gavel and stilled the room in an instant. Sally was reluctant to talk but when she noticed that both Jack and Rachel were looking at her in anticipation, and she could think of no easy way out, she surrendered. She spoke of how she met their father, Robert, during her school days.

He was a tall, handsome fellow, so she claimed, and he was quite handy in a tight spot. He was never afraid to fight if he needed to, although he had the kind of mind that could weasel his way out of trouble without the need to engage in any unnecessary entanglements. She liked him straight away but had to work hard on loving him. He seemed like a sound investment

110

because he was the kind of strong, intelligent man that she needed to keep her safe. She was emotionally fractious and insecure as a young woman and needed someone strong to lean on. Robert was a prefect and the captain of the football team, so he seemed like an ideal crutch.

She went on to explain about a young man called Neil who was a very good friend of Robert's. She fell in love with him instantly, without intent or hesitation. He was the one that made her realise that love was a spontaneous reaction, not a goal to achieve over a period of time. Butterflies celebrated in her heart whenever he walked into the room and she suspected that he too felt something similar for her. She stopped everything, momentarily, whenever she saw him. She knew he was a danger to her relationship and that Neil could end up in serious trouble with Robert if he ever found out, but the two of them took the risk anyway. They met whenever they could. To avoid getting caught, they hid their love away from absolutely everybody. After some weeks, Neil had begun to feel guilty and Sally decided that her relationship with Robert had to end. She started by refusing to join him in conversation and then by staying away from him. Sally knew now that it was childish behaviour but at the time it seemed a very logical thing to do. She distanced herself slowly over the following days. Neil kept his distance and let her dissolve her relationship at her own pace. Eventually, when her adolescent methods had failed to achieve her desired outcome, Sally had to confront Robert like an adult. Unfortunately, before she had plucked up the courage to tell him it was over, Robert had made plans of his own. Unknown to Sally and Neil at the time, he had already learned of their affair.

Robert had arranged to go fishing with Neil, which was not unusual. They often took Neil's rowing boat out onto a nearby lake, by the woods on the edge of town. Nobody suspected anything. Robert had prepared a flask of tea but had laced it with LSD. Sally was not sure how much he had put in it but it was enough to take Neil out of his senses. Robert manipulated Neil into a bad trip and turned the idyllic outing into a ferocious nightmare. Neil was hallucinating when Robert pushed him out of the boat into the lake. He was in no fit state to swim. The water was too cold and he did not stand a chance. His mind was unsure of the difference between reality and fantasy in his hallucinogenic landscape. He drowned quite quickly as Robert watched. Immediately upon his return, Robert told Sally about the incident. He openly admitted to murdering his friend and went into great detail about how he had done it. Almost poetically, he spoke of the pleading tones of his last words and the look of absolute fear in his eyes as he disappeared slowly beneath the surface of the cold, heartless lake. With great pleasure, he told the whole gruesome story as he watched Sally crumble beneath the horror of it all. She swore she could pinpoint the exact moment that her heart broke and her life had ceased to be important to her. Robert explained that he did not intend to kill Neil, only to scare him, and with sickening arrogance, admitted that the accidental death was an outcome he was prepared to accept. He knew that Sally was all but dead herself, at least emotionally, if not spiritually.

Upon realising that Sally was detached from him and beyond his power, he became violent and beat her brutally. Having nothing to lose, he threw her around the room, shouting and swearing as he slapped and kicked her. Aroused by the violence, he raped her repeatedly. He left her tattered and torn on the cold, hard floor covered in blood and bruises, wrapped in torn clothes. The diminishing silhouette in the doorway through the haze of tear-filled eyes was the last that Sally ever saw of Robert.

Several weeks later, another young fisherman found Neil's bloated corpse in the lake. The initial investigation found no suspicious circumstances and the coroner recorded a verdict of accidental death. No further investigation followed and Robert remained free. Sally had often regretted not going to the police with her side of the story, although she insisted that her doing so would have put her life in danger and the police may never have believed her anyway. From that day to this, she blamed herself in many ways for the sad demise of a much-loved young man.

She wept as she told the story. Rachel and Jack sat motionless, shocked into silence, as if in suspended animation;

feeling nothing and going nowhere with thoughtless eyes and empty hearts. Rachel was the first to snap out of her trance and stepped up to hug Sally. They cried together as Jack looked on. He was shocked. He had been conceived in the midst of a violent explosion of hatred. He felt violated, sick, and his need for a fix grew.

Soon after the emotional recital, Sally insisted she needed a drink and Rachel did not object. Jack joined her and between the two them, they finished the bottle in the kitchen cupboard and made a start on a second. In time, Sally fell asleep in her chair. Rachel tucked a crochet blanket over her legs and made sure she was comfortable. She hugged Jack. Taken aback by the gesture, he momentarily looked at her through squinted eyes beneath a furrowed brow. Rachel apologised, uncomfortably, and walked through to the kitchen to make another coffee. Jack followed after and requested tea instead. He stood nervously at the door watching Rachel as she filled the kettle and fetched the mugs from the table in the room. He began to regret not accepting the hug and felt awkward at the thought of reaching out for a second chance. His thoughts stuttered his body language and he fidgeted clumsily in the doorway.

"Yours was the blue one was it?" she asked quietly as she held up a mug.

"Yes."

"You want to get going soon? You hanging out?"

"Yes," he nodded, "but don't worry. If we go to the chemist on Grantchester Meadow I can get some clean needles. I've a got a bit of stuff for later."

Rachel stopped momentarily and looked at Jack as if she might make a comment but she said nothing, instead, she continued to make the tea. After a few uncomfortable moments, Jack felt the need to break the silence.

"I could go back to the Haven, I suppose, and get some proper help?" he spoke as if he knew he should but just needed some reassurance or encouragement to confirm his intention.

"You're being followed though aren't you? Those people you saw, are they after you?" she questioned.

"Yes. Don't worry. I can sort that out soon," Jack looked ashamed as he dropped his gaze to his feet.

"I noticed there's a guy out there now. I've seen him a few times out and about," Rachel lowered her voice as if the man outside might hear her, "I thought he was a shy punter waiting for his moment; they get like that sometimes. Never really thought anything of it until now but I swear he's following us,"

Jack went over to the window in the room and peered out. He saw the bald guy in the car, reading a newspaper. He turned to Helen.

"I don't know him. Looks like you got a stalker!" he said, trying to joke about it.

"I had one guy follow me for three months before he approached me! He's a loyal punter now, meets me at the same hotel in Leicester on the last Friday of every month. He pays for everything," she smiled, "he's a great payer. Always buys me an expensive piece of jewellery too, every time! Got me a platinum necklace once, with two diamonds and an emerald in it," she smiled to herself as she visualised the necklace in her mind's eye, "worth a bloody fortune it is!"

"He look like a punter to you?" asked Jack.

"What does a punter look like?" smiled Rachel as she shrugged her shoulders, "Never trust a stranger though, not in this game!"

Rachel shuffled some oddments in a tray on a shelf, found a pen in amongst the bits and bobs, then took an old shopping receipt from the windowsill. Looking out the window, she tried stretching left, right, and then standing on tiptoes but she could not see the registration plate.

"Take the registration of the car when we leave, just in case. But be discreet," suggested Rachel as she handed the pen and paper to Jack.

They stood in the kitchen to drink their drinks and left Sally sleeping. Jack phoned for a taxi and they left after Rachel had washed the mugs and double-checked that their mother was comfortable and safe. The man in the car looked up but did not follow them. Jack scribbled the registration number on the receipt and handed it to Rachel. When they arrived at the Haven, Jack made enquiries at the reception desk to see if he had had any visitors. The receptionist checked the logbook and confirmed that his cousin Jonny had been in looking for him and Jack was "Not to worry, he would catch up with him sooner or later."

Jack tapped his knuckles on the desk lightly and thanked the woman. He looked at Rachel and she raised her eyebrows questioningly. Jack shrugged his shoulders.

"Go get your stuff. You can stay with me for a while. At least 'til you get this sorted," she offered.

Jack disappeared upstairs for a short time. When he returned, he had a carrier bag with a few toiletries in it. He handed it to Rachel and then explained that he needed to see the Doctor in the drop-in centre. Jack disappeared again and left Rachel to her thoughts. She scanned the notice boards in the reception area and took note of the various clinics and help centres situated at various locations around the town. There were so many; smoking cessation, dieting, alcohol abuse, drug addiction, gambling and domestic violence. It made her think about all the unfortunate existences outside of her own. She considered the possibility of numerous Rachels and Jacks out there, living their disreputable lives, trapped, oppressed and lacking the wherewithal to shake off their self-destructive tendencies. She scanned across the posters again and noticed that all of them carried 'The Haven' logo and contact details.

Jack returned some time later. He smiled victoriously and nodded at Rachel as they left together. They walked through the shopping precinct, which was almost empty, as most of the shops closed an hour or so ago. The only people milling about were retail assistants and cleaners going home after another long day at work. A small group of young men stood outside a newsagent's shop across the street, drinking cheap lager, swearing at each other and spitting a lot. One of the boys stared at Jack as he passed, pointed at him and smiled at his friend. Jack looked and wondered if he was one of the gang that had attacked him. He instinctively rubbed his wound gently, which had become a dull ache. He stared on, unsure; they all looked the same in their tracksuits and caps. With growing curiosity and confidence, he strode towards the gang and the boy immediately ran off, dropping his unfinished can of lager as he did so. His friends called after him and started to walk away slowly in his direction. Jack called out and quickened his pace but the boys sped off together in a blur of verbal abuse and flying cans.

"Bastards!" whispered Jack under his breath.

Rachel waited for Jack to join her on her side of the street before they both started off together again. Jack explained about how the attack had lead to him losing the gear, and how that had lead to Kit being after him. With a sigh of relief and welcome recollection, he remembered the address that he had extracted from one of the frightened girls. Rachel was familiar with the area where the boy lived and advised Jack to give the address to Kit rather than go round himself, but he refused. The thought of being caught by Kit now, however helpful he could be in recovering the gear, was too frightening for him. He unconsciously rubbed his stitches under his jumper as he reminded himself of Kit's passion for knives. Rachel offered to deliver the message to Kit for him if he could tell her where she lived. Jack objected, but following her assertive reasoning, finally came round to her way of thinking. He agreed that the issue was best resolved quickly, and if that could be done without him actually having any contact with Kit, even better. By the time they arrived at Rachel's front door, the plan was complete, although Jack was not totally convinced. He struggled with trusting people and although he tried hard to be comfortable with Rachel, and deep down he knew he could trust her with his life, the concept was a new one to him.

Like a television presenter showing the happy contestant the new makeover they had received in their home, Rachel showed Jack round her flat. She beamed with pride; pleased that she had someone she cared about to share her achievements. They took some linen and a pillow from the cupboard in the master bedroom and made up a fresh bed in the spare room. Jack emptied his toiletries from his bag in the bathroom, taking up what little space remained on the shelves as they groaned beneath the weight of a host of golden beauty products and expensive soaps. Rachel offered to cook dinner while Jack had a shower and the pleasant evening rode into the night on the back of recited memories and light-hearted anecdotes. They were still talking at four o'clock in the morning, when Rachel decided it would be a good time to take the address round to Kit's place. She thought it best to post it while nobody was about.

"I reckon she'll still be up," Jack worried, "on something. She's probably tripping her tits off. If she isn't, she'll be shagging Jonny. She's usually up all night so you're gonna have to be quiet if you want to get away with it. Just be careful!" he warned with an obvious concern in his tone.

Rachel called a taxi and disappeared into the darkness. Jack watched the lights of the car disappear down the road and then took himself into the kitchen. He took the creased piece of foil with the gear he had taken from Mickey's and carefully opened it to reveal the brown powder. He paused for a moment, as if in prayer over a holy relic, and inhaled deeply in anticipation. With bated breath, he turned on the gas hob and took a spoon from the drawer. He reached into his inside pocket and pulled out one of the needles he had got from the drop-in. A contented smile, a relaxed sigh and he began his personalised ritual. Paranoia caused him to stop and look around the room every time he heard the slightest noise from outside. His need was growing as he neared completion but he managed to retain his patience, take his time and perform his task with expert efficiency. When the needle was loaded he cleared away and made sure he left no black traces on the spoon.

He turned off the lights and put the television in his room on very quietly before tucking himself up into bed. He discreetly removed his clothes beneath the sheets as if somebody somewhere may otherwise see his bruised and neglected naked body. Being naked in bed made him smile; he never often had the opportunity and when he did, it felt good to get his coarse threads away from his skin. He took a moment to look around the room, dimly lit in the changing light of the television screen. Even though he felt warm and wanted, he needed this fix. He injected into his thigh as he lay in his bed. By the time Rachel returned from her successful visit and popped her head around his door, he seemed fast asleep and nothing was out of place.

* * * * *

Dave had spent the early hours of the morning in Carl's car, parked opposite Sally's house, listening to Carl moan on and on about a letter he had received informing him of an unpaid fine for a littering offence. He had been complaining for almost an hour about council incompetence and the unlikely possibility of someone pretending to be him and Dave, fed up with it, was nearing the end of his tether.

"I dunno what they're talking about!" Carl said angrily, "Fucking idiots! I ought to go round their office and shove their fixed penalty notice up their arse!"

"Carl! Shut the fuck up!" Dave shook his head and rubbed his forehead as he spoke.

Carl's constant moaning was playing havoc with his hangover. He knew at the time that trying to drown out Peter's request to silence Ms Cooper with several pints of lager was a bad idea but he had attempted it anyway. He had spent the later hours of the evening with Sammy; a reliable acquaintance that worked at the Railway Station. Sammy was like Dave once, wheeling and stealing for a Mr Big figure, but he was wise enough to have escaped that lifestyle. Like a big brother Sammy was always looking out for Dave. He had tried to talk him out of his dangerous lifestyle the night before, though Dave insisted he had good reason to be in with Peter, at least until he had 'finished his mission', as he put it. Sammy knew the score, he understood Dave's position, and like a calming voice of reason in a chaotic cacophony, he offered Dave advice when he needed a much-missed conscience.

"Something's up, innit? I can tell."

"We got a situation, Carl."

Dave explained the conversation he had had with Peter while Carl was out tailing Rachel. He explained about the request to silence Sally and then to get whatever information they could from the hippies at the squat.

118

"I thought this was just a surveillance job?" questioned Carl in a worried tone, realising that things had got somewhat heavier than he liked.

"That's how it began, but something big is going on here. You don't silence people for no good reason. Not even the mighty Peter Johnson does that!"

"What do you want to do then? I mean, I don't mind wasting little tossers like Ricky, he had it coming and was no great loss, but this...."

Dave shuffled in his seat so he was facing Carl and made direct eye contact. Carl dipped his chin and fixed his gaze on Dave.

"She's just a lonely old lady," pleaded Carl.

"When I said her name, 'Sally Cooper', he went pale, Carl, dead pale!" Dave began.

Carl nodded.

"I mean, he was shaking! This woman has something on him and I think we should find out what it is. I reckon we shouldn't silence her at all - she's valuable to us. If we can't get at the stuff in the locker anymore then we're going to need something else!" Dave turned to face the dashboard. Carl nodded thoughtfully again and rubbed his chin,

"Did Sammy say anyone had been to the locker yet?"

"No mate. Whoever took the key doesn't know what they've got – if they've still got it! My guess is they burned it out in the car. I'm not gonna worry anymore about the key. If it comes to it, I'll prise the bloody thing open with a crowbar!"

"How we going to find out what this Cooper woman knows?"

"Haven't got a fuckin' clue mate!"

Dave sat and thought for a while. Carl tried hard to look as if he was thinking but he became distracted by a stray dog, jogging along the uncut privet hedging and urinating at every opportunity. Dave stared blankly at the house, the window dressings and the state of the garden. He looked up and down the row of houses and tried to imagine what kind of woman would live here, in this house, in this street. After some moments he turned to Carl,

"We try the direct approach," he said flatly, "we just ask her! Follow my lead."

Dave took the envelope of photographs from the glove compartment before he opened his door and got out the car. Carl instinctively followed. They crossed the road and made their way to Sally's house. Dave reached out and gave a firm knock at the door. Rudely awakened from her half-sleeping state, Sally sat bolt upright at the sudden banging that thudded through the house and demanded her immediate attention.

"OK. Just coming," she said in a trembling voice as she tightened her dressing gown belt around her waist.

Slowly, she pulled open the door with a shaking fist, just a little at first, but then Dave unexpectedly pushed it wide. Sally took a step back and almost lost her footing.

"Who the bloody hell are you?" she demanded, her voice still trembling.

"CID, Ms Cooper, please do not be alarmed," Dave said in an official sounding voice, "may we come in?"

The two men loomed over Sally and stepped into the hallway, obscuring what little natural light filtered in through the window on the door that Carl had shut behind him. Dave pulled a wallet from his inside pocket and flashed it at Sally as he explained that they were making routine enquiries regarding a potential criminal. In the half-light, she thought she made out an ID badge and a photograph, but her fading eyesight and the shadows made it hard for her to see it properly. She looked at the wallet and then at the two smartly dressed men towering over her. Dave returned the wallet to his pocket, tugged his collar and cufflinks and asked,

"May we take a seat and speak with you a moment please, madam? I assure you, there is no need for concern."

"Of course... ...come through," Sally surrendered as she turned and led the men into her living room, "What's this all about?"

Dave took a seat as Carl stood with his back to the fireplace and folded his arms.

"We understand that you have recently made contact with this young woman?" he asked as he showed Sally one of the photographs of Rachel.

Sally took the photograph and looked closely.

"My daughter!" she smiled nervously, "There's nothing wrong is there?" she added in a concerned tone.

"No. Please don't worry," Dave said reassuringly, "she's not in any trouble. We just need to know where she is."

"But why?"

"Please Ms Cooper, this is important. We need to know her whereabouts. We believe she is involved with a wanted criminal; unknowingly involved, that is. Do you or your daughter have any dealings with a Peter Johnson?" Dave leaned forward and retrieved the photo.

Sally sat with her mouth open for a moment and then shook her head.

"What do you want to know?" she questioned. She was getting confused and found it hard to concentrate on what he was asking her. All of a sudden her life had become uncomfortably busy and she was not sure she could cope with it. He sounded as if he had too many questions fighting her for answers.

"This girl," began Dave, "can you tell us some more about her?"

"Why?"

"Because we believe she is in possession of information that is essential to our enquiries!"

Dave began to feel his frustration rise and wondered how long he could stay calm and keep up the pretence. Carl rocked back and forth on his heels and looked down at the floor.

"Please, Ms Cooper, this is important!" he pushed impatiently.

Sally patted her thighs with her open hands and took a deep breath. She explained how Rachel had found her. She stuttered through the whole story of the separation of her children shortly after birth and their recent family reunion. She started her narrative so far back in history that Dave began to glaze over as he prayed for a snippet of information that may prove useful to him. She did not know anything about Peter Johnson other than a vague recollection of hearing his name on the radio. She did not even know what he looked like.

Dave tried hard to think of a reason why this woman would be such a threat to Peter but could find nothing. She was just a confused old woman, not as old as she looked, but still, just a lonely, scared, old woman. When Dave had learned about Rachel and Jack, he informed Sally that the investigation was undercover and that she was not to speak with anyone about this interview under any circumstances whatsoever. He emphasised the importance of secrecy in order not to hinder the investigation. He scribbled his mobile number on the back of a small card and left it on the mantle, propped up in front of the silver clock.

"If you learn anything about Rachel's dealings with Mr Johnson, please call me immediately!" said Dave in a stern, official tone.

Sally sat in silence after they had left and held her chest firmly with her hands as if to stop her galloping heart from bursting through her sternum. Dave's attempts to frighten Sally were far more effective than he could have realised. She was close to palpitations. Her vision fleetingly blurred over and her head spun as if she had stood up too fast. She found it hard to relax and her hands shook as she lit a cigarette. After a couple of draws in quick succession, she walked slowly through to the kitchen to get a drink. She came back with a glass of whiskey and left the bottle on the shelf in the cupboard.

* * * * *

With a swift kick the splintered front door flew open with a loud crack and a sudden bang as it hit the wall. The whole house seemed to jump with a startled jolt. Carl stepped in first and immediately floored the first person he saw with a swift punch to the jaw. The unconscious body fell backwards and landed sprawled across the hallway. Another young man, dishevelled and hairy, looked on through wide eyes from the doorway to the living room. He tried hard to focus on what was happening and separate his magic mushroom hallucinations from reality. The punch felt soft, like burgundy velvet and ice cream. The squelching sound of his nose breaking reminded him of the time he pulled one of his boots from the grip of the sodden mud at Glastonbury. The warmth of the blood was almost comforting and, with a smile on his face, he glided gently backwards onto the welcoming floor like a leaf zigzagging in a breeze.

Dave stepped in behind Carl and looked through to the living room. There was somebody cowering behind the couch. He could hear the shivers in her panting breath. He decided he could leave her there and go about his business. He stepped through to the kitchen as the footsteps thundered through the ceiling above him in panic. Dave looked up at where the noise was coming from. Suddenly, two young men, one after the other, landed athletically on the lawn outside before springing up quickly and running off through the broken gate.

Popper was in the kitchen, struggling to release a bolt at the top of the door to get out. He looked over at Dave with fear in his eyes. In his desperation, he repeatedly banged his weight against the door. Suddenly, the window shattered sending broken glass all over the floor both inside and out. He jumped up quick and put a leg through the window frame with the hope of climbing out but Dave had reached him and dragged him back inside. Popper shrieked as a long shard of glass jutting out from the frame tore through his flesh. His trousers were instantly soaked with blood which pulsed out of the concealed wound in time with his accelerating heartbeat.

"That looks nasty, son, better get that seen to!" whispered Dave, deliberately close to his ear.

Dave shoved Popper and he slumped down the wall as he splashed to the ground.

"Fuck you!" spat Popper, desperately clinging on to his leg and trying to stem the flow of blood.

"The girl that came here. Who was she looking for?"

"Please! Get an ambulance!" splattered Popper, growing weaker and squeezing his eyes tight shut.

"The girl!" Dave shouted.

"Fuck off!" he growled quietly through his gritted teeth.

Dave stooped to get down to eye level with Popper. He turned around quick as a shadow flicked across the wall. Someone was behind him in the doorway. For a moment, he thought that the big Mauri man had returned and the hairs on his neck stood on end with a flush of cold tingles. He felt a warm flow of relief when he saw a skinny little girl.

"Jack! She was looking for Jack! Now get him an ambulance!" screamed the girl, who stood in the doorway, trembling and crying.

Without warning, Carl turned and punched her in the chest. The force of the impact knocked the air from her lungs, lifted the frail little girl off her feet, through the hall and deposited her next to the front door.

"Woah! That was cool!" exclaimed Carl with amazement.

"You could've asked her…" grunted Dave, angry that she had begun to talk and Carl had silenced her too soon. He looked at the girl and then at Carl. Dave kneeled beside Popper and took hold of his injured leg.

"Jack who?" he sneered as he shook the leg.

Popper tried to scream but managed nothing more than a desperate whimper in the back of his throat. He was losing his vision and rapidly becoming very weak. He keeled over and became still. Dave stood up and adjusted his collar and cufflinks. He dusted down his suit as he watched the once pulsing blood from Popper's leg diminish into a feeble trickle. He realised what was happening and suddenly felt uncomfortable.

"Come on Carl. We better go," he said in a disappointed tone as he stepped away from the growing pool of blood.

Carl stood over the girl who had landed in an almost sitting position next to the splintered front door. He looked at her thoughtfully. Her hands had fallen loosely by her sides and her blouse was slightly open at the top, revealing a tempting hint of flesh.

"She's alright, you know. For a scrawny hippie chick, I mean," he said as he pulled her blouse forward so he could take a look at her small breasts.

Dave tutted and shook his head as he pushed her aside with his foot.

"Time to go, Carl, you twisted fucking pervert!"

Chapter 7

Peter mingled freely among his invited guests, with a glass of sparkling champagne and a brightly polished smile. He wandered in and out of social circles with the welcoming tones of an ever-generous host as here and there, smiling acquaintances raised their glasses and nodded their heads in his direction. Like a moth around a flame, he criss-crossed the room, seemingly at random, dropping humorous remarks into other people's conversations. He was pleased with the turnout, not so much the quality of the guests, but definitely the quantity. He knew these hangers-on would love to have had their faces seen at his grand celebration. Two local Members of Parliament and the Lord Mayor had arrived with their respective partners and Peter made an extra special fuss of them in order to gain their favour. It was an exploitative characteristic he despised to see in others but often used it himself when he knew it would reap rewards.

"No harm in greasing the wheels a little," he thought as he shook their limp hands with a fake smile.

A journalist from the local newspaper, accompanied by her photographer, followed in Peter's wake, snapping impromptu shots of small groups and couples in party gowns and tuxedos. She took names and sample quotes for the evening paper, which she carefully rephrased, to give her own professional spin to the flavour of the evening. She had phrased her well-rehearsed questions in such a way that she already knew what the answers would be, and if they differed from her expectations then she could edit them later. The photographer snapped away at random, cunningly taking selective shots of the more attractive young females for his personal collection. He took several discreet pictures of his colleague, hoping to catch a glimpse of her admiration for Peter in one of his stills so he could tease her with it back at the office. He could see that she was in awe of him. She found Peter irresistible and her adolescent flirting was almost embarrassing for him to watch.

"Hey, Mike, get a shot of those two!" she pointed discreetly at a couple at the edge of the dance floor.

They seemed to be arguing but she could not hear above the noise of the people immediately around her.

"Well spotted, Julie. What do we have here?" he smiled as he took several shots of the arguing couple.

He walked closer to them and they flickered in the flashes as if caught in a strobe light. They noticed the camera and both stared at Mike. He shrugged his shoulders with a smile,

"Just doing my job!" he said before he returned his focus to the party.

The woman, a young waitress, turned and stormed off towards the bar, muttering obscenities under her breath. The man raised his wrist and pretended to check his watch before he too walked away. Peter was engaged in conversation with a potentially influential councillor who held the 'Portfolio For Health And Education' title. They discussed how the Newbury Hall project would enhance the good work already taking place within the remit of the councillor. Effective and productive business meant reaching targets for the local administration and Peter knew it. If he could tick boxes for the council and push their political agenda they would give him a free reign and a wide berth, which is exactly what he needed.

"Your Champaign, sir," said a female voice with a sour undertone.

Peter turned to look at the interrupter and recognised the woman immediately.

"Thank you," he smiled, taking a glass from the silver tray, "Have we met?"

"You bastard!" she growled slowly through her gritted teeth.

The atmosphere around Peter changed almost immediately and the councillor found himself on the sideline of a vicious stare tinged with shades of hatred.

"I say!" objected the councillor, feeling rather awkward.

"This man…" she began slowly through her gritted teeth, pointing at Peter and talking to the councillor.

"I think this girl is drunk!" lied Peter, and he grabbed her forcefully by the shoulder and walked her away towards the toilets before she could say anything else.

The councillor was shocked and stood aghast like a fish out of water gulping for air. He embarrassingly turned to talk with other colleagues, hoping that nobody had noticed the rude display of impertinence. Just a few paces away Mike had become aware of the incident and turned his scoop-seeking camera towards the waitress.

"What the hell are you doing?" growled Peter in a whisper as he pushed her against the wall. For a fraction of a second, he felt vulnerable.

"You bastard!" she hissed, "You raped me!"

"Not so loud!" he hissed back at her, "You can't make accusations like that in here with all these people around! This is a very important evening for me! Do you know who that man is?"

"You don't give a shit do you?" she said, astonished.

"It was what you wanted. You consented to everything!"

"Fuck you! It was rape you arrogant bastard!" she started to weep in anger, "You're not above the law you know, just 'cause you've got money!"

Claire really wanted to shout but for some reason she restrained herself. She wanted others to know what he had done, she wished somebody somewhere would be within hearing distance but nobody was. The temptation to scream grew but the unlikelihood of anyone believing her word against his subdued her action.

"Now you listen here!" he snapped.

He looked back at the crowd of people around the dancefloor and made sure nobody was paying any attention. Mike saw him scan the crowd and quickly turned away before he came into his line of sight. He waited for a moment, switched off the flash then turned and zoomed in on the couple. Peter had his hand on Claire's shoulder and held her hard against the wall. The scowl on her face confirmed his suspicions that the grip was somewhat uncomfortable, if not painful. Mike reeled off several photos and then caught the attention of Julie who joined him. Peter leaned in towards the trembling waitress.

"One word from you, to anyone, and you will be just another body dragged out of the dock!" he slid his hand from her shoulder and squeezed her throat.

He stared at her for a moment as he slowly tightened his grip. She tried hard not to show him that she was struggling to breathe and that inside she was terrified and feared for her life. She wept and trembled as he released his grip. Cold needles ran across the back of her neck and down her arms. Peter stared at her with eyes as dead as a shark's. She trembled again and began to weep louder. She leaned against the toilet door and slid inside, escaping her threatening predator. Peter adjusted his collar and straightened his tie. He turned to look at his party across the room as he took a deep breath. Bathed in the flashing light of the ever-focussed camera, he returned to the dancefloor and continued to smile. Julie stood speechless and stared at Peter as he walked passed. She was seldom lost for words but right now she knew she was onto something big. As words tumbled through her thoughts she struggled to speak them; all she could do was tap Mike on the shoulder and nod slowly.

* * * * *

Rachel comforted Sally as Jack looked on, feeling useless. He hated when women cried because he never knew where to put himself or what to do. Feeling like a spare part, he stood in the centre of the room.

"When in doubt," he pondered, "put the kettle on!" and with that thought lingering pleasantly in his mind, he escaped to the comfort of the empty kitchen.

Sally eventually calmed down and Rachel sat holding her hands. Sally explained through a broken, unstructured series of paragraphs, about the two visitors that had scared her so. She explained that they wanted to speak with Rachel and she should call the number on the card that they had left by the clock.

"The police, love. What have you done?"

"Nothing Mum, I've done nothing. I don't know what they want!"

Rachel felt curious, if not a little anxious as to why they may have wanted to speak to her, but she put it to the back of her mind and concentrated on comforting her mother. They flicked on the television in time to catch the end of the local news. Sally protested and explained that she did not enjoy the television much except for nature programmes, and besides, the television was expensive now that the cost of electricity had gone up so much. The newsreader was recapping the headlines as a photo of Popper filled the screen. Rachel was startled. It was a happy picture of a younger Popper, with shorter, tidier hair and a great big smile. The happy face cut to images of the house with the scratched door and yellow tape surrounding the front lawn. Rachel raised her hand to her mother and quietened her mumbling so she could hear the television.

"And the main story tonight; a man has been found dead and two people seriously wounded in a house on the Willowdene Estate. Police are looking for two witnesses that seen running from the scene earlier today. Police suspect it is probably the work of rival drugs gangs in the area."

Rachel was shocked; she raised a hand to cover her open mouth. Her astonished eyes became damp in an instant and glistened in the light. The visiting police officers were no longer important and their questions were irrelevant.

"My God!" was all she could whisper.

Jack came in with the drinks and set them down on the table.

"Popper's dead!" said Rachel.

Jack stopped in his tracks and stared at Rachel, "What?"

"Popper's dead..." she began to weep openly.

Jack found himself standing in the middle of the room again, not knowing what to do or what to say. He knew he should be feeling something but he didn't know what. He felt empty for a second, not because his friend was dead but because he felt nothing else. Sally leaned forward,

"Who?"

130

"A friend," muttered Jack as he sat beside Rachel on the couch. He could not remember ever saying the word 'friend' out loud before and it induced a slight hint of sadness into his voice. The concept suddenly had a deeper meaning beyond the shared interest of drug use and that hit Jack hard.

"I'm sorry, mum, we've got to go," stuttered Rachel, trying to hold back her tears.

"OK," she nodded, confused.

Jack held out his trembling hand to Rachel. She took it and stood up. She kissed Sally on the cheek and gave her a little hug. Jack just nodded in her direction.

They hardly spoke to each other all the way back into town on the bus. Rachel squeezed Jack's hand tenderly for reassurance that she was not alone. He returned the gesture and rubbed her arm. Rachel felt his offer of security and smiled to herself. She stared out of the window as the dirty streets sailed by. Shop fronts replaced the terraced houses and eventually they pulled up in the town centre. Jack alighted first and Rachel followed after, stepping out into the waiting queue of people. Why they never moved aside to let the passengers off first always bothered Jack, as if they only ever did it to annoy him. He scanned the horizon in search of any potentially hostile faces to suppress his growing paranoia and noticed a young girl he knew standing by the railings. He tapped Rachel and pointed towards her.

"That's Tilly. She knows Popper!" he explained.

Rachel recognised her straight away. She had such a distinctive face; sharp, well defined features but very pretty with it.

"I've met her before," added Rachel as they both quickened their pace.

Tilly noticed the pair of them walking towards her and met them half way. She stared at Rachel with a hint of aggression in her eyes and then diverted her attention to Jack. She began to cry as she got closer. She met Jack in a hug and wept into his chest for a moment. Jack was at odds with himself again. He did not like this at all.

"What happened?" asked Rachel.

"Two guys turned up looking for you," Tilly wept as she looked up at Rachel with a hard stare.

"Looking for me?" said Rachel, surprised.

"For Rachel?" added Jack.

"Yeah. They were asking after you and what you wanted," she sobbed, "when I came round, the place was dead quiet. Everyone had left. Disco and Andy were out cold in the hallway, then I saw Popper on the floor in a pool of blood and I just ran... I was so scared Jack... I just ran...."

Jack held on to Tilly as she cried into his coat. Rachel paced up and down with her hand across her mouth.

"Why me?" she whispered.

"Why not me?" whispered Jack.

"The punter following us? The cops that went to mum's house? Are they watching me? They can't think I killed Popper can they?" Rachel pondered out loud.

"They would have arrested you straight away if they did. They would not be following you around," started Jack, "unless they think you've done something else, or you're involved in something bigger."

"Bigger than what? I haven't done anything! They must be chasing the wrong girl! I can't think of anything I've done that would attract the attention of the police and a couple of psychos!"

"They were definitely looking for you. You've brought on this trouble, wrong girl or not!" snapped Tilly, "You're gonna have to sort it out!"

"We need to think very carefully about this! Let's get back to your place and we'll suss it out," stated Jack to Rachel as he wrapped his arm around Tilly's shoulders.

* * * * *

In the bustling press office of the local evening newspaper, Julie downloaded the pictures from the camera onto her computer. She clicked through several photos of young, beautiful women in tight dresses and low cut tops. Smiling to herself, she shook her head,

"Sad, Mike, real sad!" she whispered.

She frowned as she found several pictures of her own cleavage, although she found them quite flattering,

"Cheeky sod!" she tutted, as she deleted them from the computer.

When she had found what she was looking for she nodded to herself. Several photographs of Peter and the unknown waitress covered her desktop so she could see all of the images on her monitor at once. She closed the files that were either too dark or the faces had been obscured and concentrated on just four clear images.

"Who are you?" she whispered as she tapped the glass with her long painted fingernail, "And why were you arguing with the other guy earlier on that same night?"

Mike appeared at her shoulder with a cup of coffee.

"Expresso with two, right? Anything interesting?" he asked between sips of his own drink.

"Cheers, Mike, that's lovely," she said as she took the drink, "I guess the tits and ass shots are for your collection, eh?" she asked with a smile.

Mike shook his head slowly as he dropped his gaze.

"Yeah, I should have taken them off – sorry!"

"And what's your excuse for my tits on there too?" she joked assertively.

Mike widened his eyes and held his breath. His cheeks began to redden. Julie smiled, shook her head and turned to the monitor.

"These are definitely teasing my journalistic curiosity! This here is the man of the moment, Mr Peter Johnson," she tapped the monitor again, "millionaire do-gooder, a regular saint."

"And this," she continued slowly, "is an unknown waitress at the Masonic Lodge," she paused to sip her coffee, "notice how he has hold of her in this shot? That's not saintly behaviour! That's a serious threat!"

Julie zoomed in on the image of Peter holding the waitress by the throat.

"That son-of-a-shit! You can see how scared she is!" added Mike.

"How do I adjust the image so I can see that more clearly?" asked Julie as she scrutinised the icons across the top of the screen.

Mike rested his hand over Julie's as she had hold of the mouse. He moved her hand gently and made a few clicks on the icons until the image appeared sharp and bright.

"Just like that!" he smiled smugly with his face beside hers as he hovered over her shoulder.

Julie moved her hand a little and Mike took the hint. He stood up slowly and felt slightly rejected. Julie smiled secretly to herself.

"Look at that!" she began, "Check out her eyes!"

The look of fear in the waitress's eyes was evident in the enhanced picture, and judging by the way his fingers indented the unfortunate girl's throat, it was clear that his grip was very tight.

"What is going on there?" whispered Julie.

"We need to know who the pretty waitress is, don't we?" started Mike, "I could go over and chat with her, if you like. In the line of duty of course!" he smiled.

"Yeah, right, Sir Galahad!" smiled Julie, "Like you'd do that professionally! I'll go. You get these printed and saved in our file. Nobody gets them yet!"

Julie sipped her coffee and then stood up to leave. She paused face to face with Mike as they momentarily made eye contact. She quickly looked away before the moment began to get awkward and brushed passed him with a secret smile.

* * * * *

Rachel, Jack and Tilly sat around the coffee table in subtle lamplight, hugging their steaming mugs as they stared at the table. It had taken a long time and a lot of reassurance to settle Tilly. Nobody had spoken for many long minutes. All were deep in thought. The concept of police involvement brought forward a host of fears. Should any one of them admit to being at Popper's place? How would they be implicated? The moral dilemma juxtaposed the need for self-preservation within the three individuals. The thoughts tumbled in a similar vein in the three separate minds and gathered in a mini-mass-fear between them. Paused glances and silent gazes passed across the table as if the conversation was taking place telepathically.

"Why me and not you?" questioned Rachel, suddenly breaking the silence.

The direct question severed chains of thought and herded together the wandering minds to focus on Rachel.

"They can't be Jonny's mates," concluded Jack, "or they would have been after me!"

"They don't even know you! They just said 'that girl'!" added Tilly angrily, pointing at Rachel.

"Look Tilly, I know I didn't know Popper as well as you did but I am saddened by his death. It's not my fault those guys turned up! I have no idea why they want me. Honestly," reassured Rachel.

Tilly began to cry and Jack hugged her. He rested his cheek on her head and allowed her to weep into his new jumper. After several minutes, his chest was wet and her make-up had run into the material, causing a dark smudge on the new fabric. Rachel rubbed Tilly's back and apologised. She tried again and again to reassure Tilly and console her. Tilly's anger subdued into sadness and her tears flowed freely. Rachel wept quietly while Jack remembered the good times he had with Popper. Although the tears never left his eyes, he felt as if he desperately needed to cry; not only for Popper, but also for a myriad of regrets that haunted his memories. After a long period of quiet contemplation, Tilly spoke,

"So what we gonna do?"

There was an unspoken gratitude for the broken silence and the beginning of a conversation that relieved some of the sadness and tension. Rachel and Jack shared the recent events with Tilly. They instantly trusted her as an ally and assumed she would want to help them in their search for the truth and some justice for the man who had brutally killed their friend. With all the information in the open, the three tried to tie things together. The talking crossed over from rational deduction to wild speculation and ultimately arrived at nowhere new, at which point, Rachel decided that they should eat.

"Anybody want Chinese?" she asked openly, changing the mood and hoping for a fresh start.

The change of subject was a welcome distraction that went unchallenged by the grieving friends. The left the discussion without completion and nobody wanted to reopen the case just now, although all of them knew that sooner or later, they would have some very difficult decisions to make and troublesome times ahead of them.

Rachel phoned the Golden Dragon and ordered a set meal for three with extra fried rice.

"40 minute?" confirmed the voice at the end of the telephone.

"Why is it always 40 minutes? Whatever you order, it always takes 40 minutes to get here?" questioned Rachel light-heartedly when she had hung up.

Tilly smiled and Rachel recognised an opening. The two girls made awkward small talk and attempted to get to know each other a little better as they waited for the meals to arrive. Jack sat transfixed to the television as he channel-hopped through a multitude of stations and concentrated on nothing in particular. When the doorbell rang, Jack got up and cautiously went to answer. He checked to see only one wavering outline in the etched glass window of the door before he felt confident enough to open it. Tilly and Rachel heard the muffled voices from the hallway and assumed all was well. Rachel walked through the hall to the door with the money. As the deliveryman turned to leave, Jack noticed a car parked across the street. He nudged Rachel and nodded.

"Shit!" she whispered.

Rachel and Jack went through to the kitchen with their heads bowed in silence. Tilly followed shortly after. Jack and Rachel looked up sharply the instant she appeared in the doorway.

"What?" she quizzed with a hint of suspicion.

Rachel did not want to worry Tilly and looked at Jack for support. He shrugged his shoulders and shook his head.

"I think we've been followed. There's a car outside," she said flatly.

Tilly went over to the window and pulled back the curtain a little, either seemingly at ease with or totally oblivious to the potentially dangerous situation.

"Where?" she quizzed.

Tilly peered out into the near darkness bathed in a soft orange glow from the streetlights above. There were no cars parked along the road other than in the residents' bays just outside. The glistening condensation on the bonnets indicated that the engines were cold and had been for some time. She looked across at a young couple walking arm in arm by the park and laughing with each other. Rachel and Jack peered out from over her narrow bony shoulders. The car had gone. Jack sat back on the couch with a sigh of relief. Rachel smiled and returned to the kitchen.

"And I thought I was paranoid!" whispered Tilly.

* * * * *

Claire was busily clearing glasses from a table close to the dance floor when she heard a colleague call her name. She stopped midway through lifting a glass toward her tray and turned to look where the voice had come from. Jenny was standing by the bar with another woman. They were both staring at Claire.

"Yeah?" she asked after a slight pause.

"This is Julie Moore from the Evening Telegraph. She wants to speak with you."

Claire joined them at the bar then passed the tray of glasses to her colleague who took them into a back room.

"What you after?" asked Claire with a hint of defensive aggression.

"We're running an article on Peter Johnson and his new drug rehabilitation project. It's big news for the town and he's hot at the moment. I wondered if you had anything you would like to tell us?"

Julie spoke with a raised intonation toward the end of each sentence as if everything she said was a question. Claire cringed inwardly when she heard it and took an instant dislike to this intrusive woman.

"What do you think of Mr Johnson?" she asked again before Claire could get a word in.

"Why ask me? I'm no druggie and I don't even know the guy! He holds his parties here, and I just happen to work here. End of!" she said angrily as she stepped away.

Julie reached out and took Claire by the elbow.

"I saw you arguing with him the other night," she raised a finger to point out the red marks on Claire's neck, "we just want to hear your side of the story," she asked directly.

"Piss off!" she scowled in reply.

Claire marched off with a frown and disappeared into the Ladies toilets. She slammed the door behind her but the sprung loaded hinge disappointingly muted the satisfying bang she anticipated. Julie followed her in quickly.

"I don't like him either you know!" she called through the cubicle door, deliberately changing tack as if to take sides with Claire, "he strikes me as a bit of an arrogant bastard, really! A bit up himself. Always wants his own way."

There was no reply from the cubicle but Julie could hear Claire sniffing slightly. After a moment the flush sounded. Julie stepped back from the door as Claire stepped out towards the hand basins. She turned the tap on with such a hard twist that the water shot out at speed and immediately launched itself up the side of the basin and down her apron.

"Shit! Now look!" she groaned.

"Please…" started Julie

Claire swung round and grabbed Julie by the collars of her coat. She pushed her hard against the supporting wall of the cubicles behind her and fixed her with a stare that turned Julie cold. Julie usually knew when to surrender and not to push any further, but this time she had totally misjudged the situation and gone too far.

"Piss off and leave me alone!"

Claire's voice was ferocious as she scowled at Julie with their noses almost touching. She let go with a shove and Julie stumbled back into a cubicle. It was only a fortunate grab of the toilet roll dispenser that saved her from falling any harder onto the toilet. By the time Julie had got out of the Ladies', Claire was busy at the tables again.

* * * * *

Sally awoke in the early hours of the morning; it was still dark outside. As the realisation of what had happened the night before settled in her memory, she felt ashamed of herself for finishing the bottle of whiskey and not going to bed. Her neck hurt, but no more than usual. An empty bottle lay on the floor at her feet; the television played away to itself with the sound turned off. Puzzled, she tried hard to remember why she had switched it on in the first place. Slowly, she pulled herself up from her chair, cautiously so as not to annoy the aches and pains that riddled her ageing limbs. She reached out to turn the television off. Her outstretched fingers were millimetres away from the button when a familiar face filled the screen.

She stopped. The room around her stopped. The world around her room stopped. Her reality juddered to a halt in sections, like carriages on a train when they meet suddenly with a buffer at the end of the line. Everything ceased to exist except the photograph of the man on the television, which had expanded to fill her vision. Sally was distraught. An evil being had entered her house, bringing with it a nightmare she had thought was long since dead. The demon had aged, his face had wrinkled and his hair had greyed but she could still see the same monster looking back at her. It was without a shadow of doubt the man that had drowned her lover. A sudden build up of pressure forced Sally back into her chair and hammered into her chest. The sensation was little more than a dull ache at first but very quickly accelerated into an unbearable pain that gripped her tight and squeezed her insides with an iron fist. Her lungs tried desperately to expand in order to fill with air but the contracted

139

muscles between her ribs locked tight. Sally's eyes bulged and her mouth became dry. Her tongue swelled as her throat went into spasm and pushed her head forward. Her arm cramped and her hands clenched so hard her fingernails dug deep into her sweating palms. The pain was consistent, like rolling thunder ploughing through her soiled soul, striking lightening through her heart, without mercy. For several, long, frightening moments, Sally was held in a deadly embrace, helplessly clutching her chest and gasping for release, desperately hoping that it was not her death that came to rescue her from her suffering.

Chapter 8

Tilly stood in front of Jack and Rachel like an officer addressing her troops, as she tried desperately to talk them into luring their follower out into the open. She was convinced it was the only way they could find out who it was and what he wanted. She had thought about her options and had decided that it was better for Rachel to face the threat head on and get it over with than live in fear of the unknown.

"If we go somewhere public, in the open with lots of people around, we'll be OK!" she said reassuringly.

"Yeah right!" laughed Jack sarcastically as he nestled further back into the comfort of the cushions on the couch.

"It is a bit iffy, Tilly. This bloke is probably dangerous!" Rachel shrugged.

"But in the open? With people around?" Tilly walked round in a small circle then leaned forward over the coffee table.

"And if the cops are after you, they might already know the guys that did Popper!" she stood upright and raised her hands in front her.

To Tilly, this was all logical deduction. It had no risk attached and she could not work out why the two siblings had to show such resistance to her plan. She walked around the room so much that Jack found it hard to follow her without losing attention. He was still tired and the absence of heroin in his system was beginning to niggle at him. She gesticulated with her hands when she spoke and her face painted the words for all to see. She had all the enthusiasm and excitement of a five-year-old child on Christmas Eve, which only added to Jack's nervousness.

"You know it makes sense," she nodded, "and besides, if they wanted you dead, they'd have got you by now. And if that copper wanted to arrest you, well, he's had plenty of chances by now hasn't he?"

She stood still with her hands on her hips and smiled an 'I win' smile. Jack and Rachel knew that they could not argue a reasonable case against her, although both of them wanted to.

"Where?" surrendered Rachel.

141

"I dunno!" said Tilly as she joined them on the couch, "Café or pub or something, somewhere public and open, with an outside."

"Noble's," said Jack flatly.

* * * * *

Dave watched the three friends as they sat around a coffee table outside of a street café. Carl sat in the driving seat, as usual, with his redtop open at the topless model page.

Rachel was sitting back in her chair with one hand wrapped around her cup on the table; the other casually leant on the back of the empty chair next to her. She had her legs crossed at the knees, which had lifted her skirt a little to reveal her excellent thighs and her accentuated calves complimented by her high heeled shoes. Dave followed the leg with his lingering gaze from the tanned ankle upwards until her clothing spoiled the view. Jack sat hunched over a coffee, which he continuously stirred with a thin wooden stick. He looked up now and again when Tilly spoke or he noticed an attractive girl passing by, but most of the time he stared into his drink and shuffled his feet beneath his chair. He did not want to be outside, it made him feel exposed and vulnerable. His body trembled slightly, beneath his skin, and his muscles were beginning to show the early signs of cramp. Withdrawal was setting in and he was powerless to stop it, however hard he tried to block the thoughts out of his mind, he could not deny that he needed a fix. Tilly sat upright with her arms folded. Her back was straight and her face fixed in a non-descript manner. Only her eyes moved to follow the passers by. Now and again, when something or someone caught her interest in the street, she burst from her posture and metamorphosed into a playful girl with lots to say about whatever-it-was that had summoned her enthusiasm. Rachel admired her childlike quality and charm. Tilly could get excited about the most trivial of things. She toyed with a sachet of sugar for a while and delicately emptied the contents onto the wrought iron table. She artistically piled the sugar on the curves of the ironwork and then gently pushed it all through the holes with the empty sachet, which she had folded, very neatly, into a sort of spoon. Rachel smiled to herself as she watched Tilly play. She was miles away. Miles away from Rachel and Jack and the man in the car they knew was following them. Maybe it was her childlike charm and innocence that had lead Rachel to agree to setting this trap but now it was real and not just an idea, she was beginning to doubt her plan. She could see Jack's tension all around him like a grey aura, shrouding him in anxiety and nervousness. Tilly seemed unaware that this situation could get dangerous; it was nothing more than an exciting game for Tilly. How could Rachel have ended up here, exposed, like bait for the on-looking predator?

"Alright Jack?" hissed a voice from Jack's left.

He turned to see Kit walking towards him, flanked by Jonny and the third man that he did not know. Kit stood behind Jack as the unknown man pulled a chair from a nearby table and sat next to Rachel. He smiled as he admired her legs. Rachel tutted and turned away from him as she stretched her skirt down a little.

"Jack?" nodded Jonny as he sat down next to Tilly.

Tilly froze and looked at him from the corner of her eye.

"Fancy finding you here, Jacky boy!" said Kit as she began to massage his shoulders.

Jack felt uncomfortable and started to tap his feet rapidly. He rubbed his hands together and tried to focus on Tilly who just stared at him with an expression somewhere between fearful and excited.

"You're so tense Jack! What's the matter with you then?" asked Kit sarcastically.

In the car across the street, Dave nudged Carl and pointed at the three that had now become six. Carl folded his paper onto the dashboard and bobbed his head to look across at their mark.

"Who do you think that might be?" asked Dave.

Jack could not help but enjoy the massage; it offered a slight relief from his growing aches. Kit had an excellent touch and was working Jack's back and neck just right. Within the pleasure, he could sense her sinister bullying and he could not stop his paranoid mind from twitching.

"You lost my gear, Jack," she began slowly and clearly, "which is a bad thing. Now I'm sorry you took a knife for it and I'm thankful to you for letting me know where it was, but," she paused for effect, "you lost my gear!"

"What?" started Jack.

Kit pushed her thumbs hard into Jack's spine and he curled backwards in discomfort. Rachel leaned forward a little but the third man pushed her back in her seat.

"Sit down, shut up, stay still!" he sneered in a threatening tone.

Rachel frowned and shook her head.

"Grow up! Tosser!" she whispered.

The man got up and stood over Rachel in a failed attempt to frighten her.

"Sit down, Tony. Don't make a scene!" advised Jonny, as he scanned the nearby diners and passers-by.

"Sit!" snapped Rachel as if training a dog, "Don't make a scene!" she mimicked.

Tony sat down again and sneered at Rachel. Rachel sneered back. Jack was worried that Rachel's defiance to the intimidation may provoke an attack or get them into more trouble. A cold chill ran through his stomach. He shook his head slowly in her direction. Rachel silently shrugged her shoulders in response.

"You a big strong girl are you love?" asked Kit as she rubbed Jacks upper arms, "You think you got what it takes do you?"

"What do you want, Kit?" interrupted Jack, "You got your stuff back so what you after?" he quizzed, hoping to end this meeting quickly.

"It wasn't all there when I got it, thanks to you, Jack! Now either you and that maggot Mickey took some or those chavs sold it on before I got to it," she explained.

She stopped rubbing him and held his arms in a tight grip.

"Which is it?" she demanded as she lowered herself down to his ear.

"Those kids must have got it, Kit, not me or Mickey. You know we wouldn't rip you off," he said in a friendly, obedient tone, hoping to get her on his side.

Jack's mind flitted quickly and an idea suddenly struck him. The speed of the thinking surprised Jack, but he had no time to congratulate himself. His mouth automatically began speaking before he felt ready to talk.

"I've got to tell you," he began, "I'm being followed and we're being watched right now!"

Kit remained perfectly still. Jonny and Tony sat upright and scanned the area like startled meerkats.

"In that car across the street; the two blokes there. See 'em?" Jack waited for a nod from Jonny, "They're coppers and they've been onto me for a while. They don't know that I know they're there, but I do."

Jack tried hard to sound ominous. Kit turned around slowly and scanned the road. Sure enough there were two smartly dressed men in a Jaguar and they looked suspiciously like police officers of one kind or another. As Jack had hoped, Kit's fear of authority and men in suits forced her onto the back foot and invoked her paranoia.

"Don't look, Kit! They don't know you do they?" he continued in his friendly, concerned tone,

"They don't have your photo yet, but if you look over, they might get one. Probably got a camera trained us as we speak!"

"Oh great!" shrugged Kit, "What do they want?"

"That gear was marked!" Jack lied, "and they're onto it. It was cut with something cold and its put people in hospital!" he added, hoping they could not tell that he was lying.

Jack had the plan unfolding in his mind and his imagination ran with the story. It would only sound credible if he did not take it too far. He had to know when to stop. He had to hold back some of it, just enough to keep her paranoid. Kit would not try anything with the police watching and he knew Jonny had served time before.

"Best you leave now, Kit, and take your pals with you. I wont be seeing you again now will I?" said Jack in a brave tone that kept his real fear well hidden.

Jonny looked at Tony and they nodded to each other. They stood up slowly and nodded to Kit.

"I'm not going inside again, Kit, not even for you!" Jonny whispered, "I'll go check this out!" he added calmly.

He leaned over and gave Kit a tender kiss on the cheek. She turned to kiss him in return but he had stepped away. The two men walked slowly down the street away from the group and crossed the road near the end at a T-junction.

"Looks like your pit-bulls have left you standing!" Tilly joked.

"Piss off Rat Face!" Kit sneered.

Tilly sat back, folded her arms and crossed her legs. She turned sideways and scowled. Tony and Jonny were soon out of sight. Kit suddenly felt stranded and defenceless. Her sinister, threatening demeanour changed and she became more friendly and civil. She turned to sit with Rachel and asked her name. Rachel showed her defiance by turning slightly away and crossing her legs away from her.

"You can't come here all threatening and then turn on the charm just 'cause you're boyfriend bombed you out!" Rachel jeered, "Piss off under whatever rock it was you crawled out of and don't bother us again!"

Kit apologised for her earlier attitude and continued to question Rachel. Her voice tinged with a hint of nervousness and Jack could see that she almost squirmed. After some time avoiding Kit's verbal probing, Rachel pointed out towards the car with a startled expression on her face.

Jonny was leaning into the driver's side window and shouting something at the driver. It was difficult to make out the exact words but they were definitely arguing about something. Tony stood on the other side of the car with his arms against the roof above the door. He too was shouting something at the passenger. Several shoppers had begin to avoid the area and had started to cross the road or turn back on themselves as they approached the trouble. The two large men

146

pushed the roof of the car and it rocked side-to-side. Jonny tugged at the car door but it would not open. Tony kicked the passenger door with a loud thud. The voices got louder and without warning a gunshot rang out. The town instantly became still for a moment until suddenly, another shot filled the air. A scream broke out among the frozen crowd, followed by another two gunshots. The sharp sound of terror echoed from the shop walls like the crack of a deadly whip. The crowd scattered and people shouted. Rachel and Tilly stood up in disbelief. With a screech of wheels and a small wisp of smoke, the car sped off out of sight as passers by ran from the scene.

The street was in pandemonium. People screamed and shouted. They ducked into arcades and scattered off down side streets. Cars had stopped in their tracks and shop doors slammed shut behind fleeing customers as they ran for cover. From a block-paved area of the shopping precinct jogged a police officer on foot, talking into his radio as he neared the commotion. After a few moments of panic, the distant sound of a wailing siren pierced the air. All that remained on the pavement across the street was the fallen body of Jonny and a few onlookers that were either too stupid or too scared to leave. Tony had gone. Kit stood shocked. Her mouth had dropped open and her glistening eyes grew damp. Frozen to the spot, she quivered, as tears became frequent. Her stomach went into spasm and she jolted forward with every short burst of crying as the unstoppable emotion spewed from her body. Rachel took Jack by the shoulder and pulled him towards her.

"Time to leave!" she said quickly.

Rachel, Jack and Tilly disappeared with the fleeing crowd and left Kit alone among the scattered seats and toppled tables, transfixed on the motionless body of her lover.

They did not follow the crowd for long. In a few short minutes they were out of harms' way and separated by the pushing and shoving of strangers. They regrouped at a bus shelter and caught their breath. Rachel felt thrilled at the excitement and smiled to herself. Jack ran his fingers through his hair and paced up and down the length of the shelter. Tilly leaned forward with her hands on her knees as she breathed loudly and heavily. She eventually looked up and smiled at Rachel.

"Wow!" she gasped, "What a rush!"

Jack shook his head,

"This is not a good thing! How can you be enjoying it?"

He rubbed his wound as he paced and shook his head in disbelief. Now and again, he lightly punched the plastic windows of the shelter.

"Way I see it," Rachel gasped between breaths, "is we either enjoy the ride... or... we buckle under the stress!"

"Yeah, me too," added Tilly, "I'm telling ya, Jack, if I wasn't laughing about this, I'd be a snivelling wreck!"

Jack was confused; he had no idea how he was feeling. It could have been fear or excitement but it had been so long since he had experienced any energetic emotions that he had forgotten how to express them. He stopped pacing long enough to pull a cigarette from his pocket and he offered one to Tilly. They lit up from the same match and inhaled deeply.

"We should get home," said Rachel as she peered out from the shelter, as if she was hiding from someone.

The three friends very cautiously crept out of the shelter and scanned their surroundings. Everything had seemed to return to normal. People had started to meander down the street toward the scene, totally unaware of the events that unfolded just moments before their arrival. Another feint siren grew louder and a police car flashed passed the end of the street toward the scene, followed by another and then by an ambulance.

* * * * *

Kit was still standing outside the café as if she was not in the same dimension as the goings on around her. She had been rooted to the spot in fear and in shock. Her eyes fixed on where Jonny's body lay, but the fluorescent yellow jacket of the paramedic that was attending to him obscured her line of sight. The police had taped off the area and were pushing the onlookers back away from the scene. Several other officers were asking questions of the people that stood closest to where Jonny had fallen. One officer crossed Kit's line of sight as he placed yellow plastic markers on the road where the tyres had left black marks. Another had begun to take photographs. Kit was oblivious to everything around her. She could see it, hear and feel it but none of it registered. Her senses were working overtime although her mind had become detached from everything else but Jonny. She watched as the two paramedics lifted him onto a stretcher. A clear tear crept down her cheek and she blinked for what she thought was the first time since she heard the gunshots. The paramedics pulled a sheet over his body and held aloft a drip bag as they wheeled him into the waiting ambulance with a great deal of urgency. Kit broke down and fell to her knees with her head in her hands.

"Nooo!" was all she could scream.

She sobbed loudly into her hands as her world crashed down around her. Bitter emotions poured out of her fractured soul in a puddle of vomit. She fell forward and leaned on her arms, instinctively avoiding the bile. The distinctive sharp scent hit her nostrils and she puked again. She sat in her sadness, staring down at her vomit, and for the first time heard the noise all around her. She became dizzy and overcome with her chaotic surroundings. Her vision blurred and she was sick again. She felt a gentle something on her shoulder that at first did not register. Gathering her thoughts, she slowly looked up. A police officer stood over her and offered her support.

"Are you OK miss? Can I help you at all?" he questioned politely.

Kit said nothing. She wiped her mouth on her sleeve and stood up slowly. She looked at the officer and sneered.

"Are you OK miss?" he repeated.

Kit spat in his face and turned to run. She bumped into one table and fell awkwardly against another. The officer wiped his face and started after Kit but he stumbled on an upended chair and landed on the floor. Kit was the first to her feet and ran off as fast as she could. Her vision blurred through her teary eyes but she could see enough to avoid any further obstacles. The heavy plodding footsteps of the pursuing officer faded away as she gained speed and disappeared into a side street. She continued to run across a road, down an alleyway, passed the girls' school and down Old Station Road. She stopped when she reached the boarded up train station and came to rest against a graffiti-covered wall. After a few minutes catching her breath, she registered where she was and leaned around the corner to look down the street.

* * * * *

"The two killers are the same one's that are following you, aren't they?" asked Jack in a scared tone, "it's the same fucking people!"

"They've got to be bent coppers I reckon!" said Tilly.

"Makes sense, I guess," added Rachel, "but why are they after me?"

"It's got to be a drugs thing. Bent coppers always get involved with drugs!" added Tilly.

"Scary shit!" whispered Rachel.

Jack just shrugged and rubbed his wound.

"I feel sick," he said in a downward tone, "I'm done in and I need a fix!"

Rachel just gave him a look and he knew exactly what she meant by it.

"Got nothin' Jack. What about you?" asked Tilly, being deliberately defiant against Rachel's non-verbal, moral opinion.

"Nothin'," he lied. He remembered he had a small amount leftover from the powder he had stolen from Mickey but it was not enough to share. He thought it best not to admit to it so he would not disappoint.

"I got a bit of weed, Jack," said Tilly as she pulled a penny bag full of bush out of her pocket, "we can share a spliff when we get back home."

"Not in my place you won't!" said Rachel, disgusted, "You take that shit outside if you must have it at all!"

Jack and Tilly looked at each other and smiled as Rachel walked up the steps to her front door. When she stepped into the living room, she screamed a short, sharp scream. Jack and Tilly came running in behind.

"I'm sorry," said Dave, "I have to speak with you!" he added, as he stood up with his palms downward in a peaceful gesture.

He paused to register the reaction as he took a deep breath.

"How did you get in?" Rachel asked.

"I have my own key," he replied as he raised a selection of metal lock-picks on a keyring from his jacket pocket.

"Who are you?" asked Jack, slightly nervous.

"I work for Peter Johnson," began Dave, "and he asked me to keep tabs on Rachel here."

"You? Me? Why?" asked Rachel, puzzled.

Tilly had sneaked into the kitchen and returned with a large knife, which she held out in front of her as she entered the room.

"You killed Popper you bastard!" she growled through her increasing tears, "I saw you there!"

"That was an accident – I swear! I never meant to hurt him!"

Dave explained how Popper had tried to climb out through the window. He held up his hands towards Tilly as a sign of defence as he spoke calmly to Rachel and Jack.

"He must have hit an artery or something!" he suggested.

"You could have called an ambulance!" she hissed as she stepped forward slowly.

Rachel was becoming concerned for Tilly. She knew she would not stand a chance in a confrontation against Dave; he could snap her like a toothpick if he chose to, and he was probably armed.

"Hear him out, Tilly. Let's just hear him out first," whispered Rachel as she stepped out in front of her.

Tilly shivered and shook her head slowly. The tears on her cheeks reflected the light from the shimmering silver blade as her hands trembled.

"I'm not any kind of threat!" said Dave as he opened his jacket and placed a gun on the coffee table in front of him.

He took a step back with his hands raised. Jack reached out slowly to take it.

"But I wouldn't do that if I were you," Dave said in a calming tone, "that piece just killed a man. You don't want your prints on there now do you?"

Jack stepped back and Dave sat on the arm of the chair across from the sofa. Tilly shivered as she held the blade in front of her. She began to buckle, as her legs became weak. Jack wrapped his arms around her as she fell to her knees and dropped the knife. He held her as she cried and slid the knife under the sofa out of harm's way.

"You're the bloke that's been following us. What you want me for?" asked Rachel as she walked round the sofa and took a seat on the arm, being cautious not to sit any lower than Dave had for fear of intimidation.

"I don't know! I thought you wanted Mr Johnson."

"I don't really know him. I mean, why would I want him? He's got nothing I want."

"Then what's it all about?" interrupted Jack.

"Johnson is concerned that you are looking for him and he wanted to know who you are and what you do. Thing is, you're not after him are you?"

"No," she shrugged.

"But he knows your mother, Sally Cooper. When I mentioned her name to him he reacted big time. He even suggested she be silenced."

Jack stood up and supported Tilly onto the sofa. He sat her down and handed her a cushion. He stepped forward,

"Now wait a minute," he began, "why do you want our mum?"

"It's OK, hotshot, I'm not going to touch her! Besides, I think she's more useful alive than dead!"

"What?" snapped Rachel, "What are you talking about? I met Pete Johnson one night as a client and he didn't have the balls to go through with it!"

Rachel paused, then remembered,

152

"He left before he did anything but we still took his money! Maybe that's it!"

"No. I doubt that," Dave shook his head, "he's got more money than you can imagine and he wouldn't worry about the few measly quid he paid you."

Rachel frowned, as she suddenly felt belittled and cheap.

"But he knows you, somehow," pondered Dave, "and your mother."

Tilly had sat down on the end of the sofa and had watched the conversation fly back forth as if she were watching a game of tennis. Her eyes were wide and she did not have a clue what was going on or why this man was in Rachel's flat. It was as if the last few moments had not happened and had been totally deleted from her memory. She noticed that both Rachel and Jack had fixed their gaze on Dave and were showing no recognisable signs of fear. Tilly joined them. He tugged at his collar and cuffs and leaned forward.

"Peter Johnson is a nasty piece of work. Not a lot of people know him as I do. He worked his way up through the drugs market; buying and selling; import and export, for years."

Dave paused. He could see he had their full attention.

"There never was a lottery win; he made his money with dope… coke… heroin… and any other filth he could push!" he sat back and appeared to relax a little.

"He got his fingers burned in a couple of deals and decided he wanted out. He thought he'd be better off away from the front line and took a new role in the same business. He got fools like me to work for him," he sighed,

"He recruits addicts and dropouts from his Haven foundation. Promises them the world and they're so hopeless they take him up on it. They're expendable, see? If they get caught, he denies all knowledge and nobody can touch him. Who'd ever believe a junkie over him?" he leaned forward again and rested his elbows on his knees.

"He even changed his name so he could appear to go straight and wipe out his history. He became the lottery-winning businessman that everyone respects. Sickening, innit?" he gesticulated as he spoke.

153

"I worked with him for a while, buying and selling to the dealers, small time, mostly. I got off H quite early," he continued, "when my social circle started to disappear. I avoided too many funerals in those days. Sad really," Dave looked up for a moment and then continued, "I found out Johnson was cutting his gear with all kinds of shit and it was getting dangerous. By that time he was the number one supplier in town and his gear was threatening the lives of every addict this side of the river! He had to be stopped but his organisation was too big. He was too powerful."

"This is crazy stuff!" Jack whispered as he shook his head.

"So he sells the gear to create the addicts and then offers them rehab?" questioned Tilly, looking very puzzled.

"So he can skim a little cream off the pudding! He can double his money embezzling in his so-called charity and selling shit to junkies!"

"What a bastard!" whispered Jack.

"Go on…" beckoned Rachel.

"Well, I cleaned up my act and kept an eye on Johnson. I infiltrated his trust. I monitored his every move and learned his ways. I know that man's secrets and how he thinks, and I swore that I would bring him down, one day, from the inside."

Dave tugged at his collars and cuffs again and shuffled in his seat.

"I've got a shit load of evidence; photos, papers, receipts, change of name deed, even a video clip; safe and sound in a locker at the station, but I can't get at it. The key has been…" he paused and rocked his hands, "misplaced, and besides, there's not enough evidence on its own. I need more. I need the missing link."

Rachel remembered the key she had found in the car and wondered. She opened her mouth to question Dave but thought better of it. She did not know where her trust was at the moment and so thought it would be better if she kept that particular card close to her chest for the time being.

"I know your mother is the key to all this. She can put this scum away where he belongs! Can you help me?"

* * * * *

Mickey tinkered with the tools of his trade on the lid of his box as Kit paced up and down the room in tears. She tried phoning the hospital again but they refused to give her any information about Jonny unless she told them who she was and her relationship to him. She was not prepared to do that because of her fear and distrust of authority. Every time they denied her request, she growled a scream into the phone and flipped it shut in anger. Mickey felt safe with her being scared and fragile. He was pleased that Jonny was down and Tony had disappeared although he did not admit it to himself, let alone show it to Kit. They had both been a burden to Mickey and he secretly hated them. They were mindless bullies and had made Mickey's miserable life even harder to bare over the past three-and-a-half years. Kit was no longer a threat to him in her present state and he actually felt sorry for her, regardless of how she had treated him before. He looked up and handed her a loaded syringe.

"Fresh today!" he said, "This'll bring you round!"

She stood motionless and stared down at the offering. A thousand tiny beads of sweet temptation tumbled through her mind and created one focal point of need. She reached out slowly and sat down quickly. Within minutes there were two reclined bodies in Mickey's living room. One sprawled out across the couch and the other slumped back in an armchair; both of them wrapped in an infinite comfort of love and warmth. Deep within their veins flowed the stuff of dreams as it spiralled through their essence and steered their senses towards their own personal paradise. While the two heavenly souls floated obliviously in their own celestial bliss, a heavy, thorny claw lowered itself slowly around their hearts and squeezed. A thick, black tar polluted the platelets and plasma in their veins and slowly, deliberately, dragged their dreaming souls down into the fiery depths of hell. They could offer no resistance. Their rainbows faded to grey. Their sun desiccated as it crumbled to ash. Their pulsating hearts ceased to beat and cramped their valves tight shut. Their minds ceased to wander. Their bodies lay motionless and infinitely empty.

* * * * *

Rachel took Dave's number that he had scribbled on a piece of paper before he left and stored it in her phone. Tilly came through from the kitchen with hot drinks and a plate piled high with buttered toast.

"It's all I could find. You got no food in. When do you ever shop?" asked Tilly sarcastically.

"I eat out a lot – perk of the job!" smiled Rachel.

The humour was tinged with avoidance. There was a lot of confusion in the air and the friends were all scared, but none of them wanted to show it. Nobody was prepared to confront the fear. Rachel fumbled in her handbag looking for the key she had taken from the stolen car. She emptied several slips of paper, a packet of condoms and a selection of make-up onto the coffee table, but no key. She jumped up and paused with her hand in her hair. Suddenly, she was off again, swift and sure through to her bedroom.

"You all right there, Rachel?" questioned Jack.

"Just got... to... ah! There you are!" she said from out of sight.

She returned to the room holding aloft a small key on a fob.

"I bet you a pound to a penny that's the locker Dave was on about!" she smiled.

Tilly had opened one of the condoms and was stretching it out over her hand. She seemed fascinated by the feel and the look of her skin pressed tight against the lubricated latex. She smiled to herself and she pulled it this way and that to distort her view.

"Can you really tell it's got these ribs on when it's inside you?" she asked openly as she toyed with the textured surface.

Suddenly, the condom shot across the table towards Jack. Tilly laughed. Jack shook his head disapprovingly.

156

"We should go there," started Rachel, "and get this evidence Dave's got stashed away!"

"Sure?" questioned Jack.

"He doesn't know it's us that has the key does he? Just a spot of luck! Small world innit?" she smiled.

"Dead small!" agreed Jack.

Jack and Tilly reluctantly agreed. As soon as the toast was little more than a scattering of greasy crumbs, Rachel called for a taxi. Their fear was laced with excitement and gave them the motivation and determination they needed to embark on their quest. They travelled in tense silence. Rachel sat in the front. The driver had attempted to make conversation but the reply was short and cutting so he did not bother again. Within fifteen minutes they were at the New Central Train Station. Rachel lead the way and Tilly trotted up behind. They stood beneath the overhead signposts and craned their necks to get an idea of which platform was where.

"Platform 4: Over the bridge," said Jack as he jogged off towards the stairs, "this way…"

Rachel and Tilly followed after. Jack skipped up the stairs two-in-a-stride while Rachel and Tilly took their time. He waited at the top of the stairs looking down at them with a wry smile.

"Girls never do that do they?" he asked rhetorically.

They found the platform easily enough but the lockers were a little harder to locate. The platform was a long one with kiosks and heavily laden baggage carts obscuring the view here and there. Eventually Jack shouted out and the two girls headed off to the direction of the voice, hidden behind a flower stall.

"What number?" asked Jack, "This is 130's to 160's here. They go that way," he pointed.

The lockers lined the wall for quite a distance and curled off around a corner further down.

"302. Miles away!"

They did not see that as they walked along the row of metallic doors a guard on the far side of the platform paid close attention. He stood with his hands behind his back and followed their every move until they came to a halt at locker 302.

It was on the bottom row and Rachel had to kneel with one knee on the platform to get at the contents. As soon as the door was open, Sammy took out his mobile phone.

Rachel reached in and took out a battered, red biscuit tin. It was a square one with a faded picture of the contents on the lid. She prised it open and sifted through the paperwork inside. She pulled out a photograph and showed it to Jack. It was Peter with two other men. He was holding a small briefcase and one of the other men had a similar case. They were swapping. It reminded Rachel of the kind of photos that private detectives take when they follow someone for a client. Rachel sifted back through the box and found four other photographs, all taken in sequence with the first.

"Dodgy dealings!" she whispered.

"Dave will know who these other guys are, no doubt," said Tilly.

"Hope so, or this is no use to us is it?" added Jack.

Rachel sealed the lid and checked the locker one more time. There was a videocassette pushed to the back, almost out of sight. She slipped into her bag as she turned to go. Jack and Tilly followed. Sammy, still watching from the far end of the platform, returned his phone to his pocket.

The journey home was a quiet one, with a concealed feeling of growing excitement that only made its presence known through subtle fidgets of nervousness and anticipation. Rachel sat in the front of the taxi with the box on her lap, holding it as if it contained something precious. Jack and Tilly stared at the box throughout the entire journey. The taxi-driver became slightly suspicious and gave Rachel many sideways glances as his gaze drifted from the road to the box and back to the road. Rachel sensed his uneasiness and smiled a polite smile,

"Family heirlooms," she nodded, "not a bomb or anything!" she added jokingly.

The taxi driver just smiled and nodded as he began to drive a little faster. Back at the flat, Rachel took all the papers from the tin and arranged them across her dining table where she had enough space to see most of the sheets at the same time. She put the photographs in one pile and the slips of paper in another. There were a series of receipts and a photocopied tax return, together with a few P60s, which she piled together in date order. It seemed that Dave had been right in thinking there was not enough proof to secure a conviction, although a lot of this evidence put together would certainly damage Peter's reputation. It may even give the police a reason to investigate his dealings further. However disappointed, Rachel continued to make sense of the story as it unfolded before her. There were several loose sheets of very floppy paper, creased and dog-eared between the thicker A4 sheets. She flattened out the paper and realised that it was from a fax roll.

"Clever bugger!" she whispered to herself, "I bet you faxed these out of the office while he was in the next room or somewhere, didn't you Dave?"

She saw that one of the faxed sheets was a copy of a 'Change of Name Deed' dated and signed by a solicitor, with an official looking stamp at the top. Some of the lettering was hard to make out because of the creases but she could see that Peter Johnson was actually born Robert Harrison.

"No fuckin' way!" she exclaimed to herself.

She quickly shuffled through other scraps of fax rolls and found more letters in the name of Robert Harrison. She paused and took a deep breath. Her mobile phone began to ring from her handbag out in the other room and immediately gained her attention. She walked through to the living room and retrieved the phone. Jack was licking a cigarette paper and had every intention of sticking it to the others in his hand to make a larger sheet. Tilly was removing the dry tobacco from a cigarette onto the table.

"Not in here! Take it out back, please!" said Rachel in a stern voice as she answered her phone.

"I'll skin up here and then we'll go out," said Jack, looking up to Rachel, "It's windy out there!" he reasoned.

Rachel had begun to cry and covered her mouth with her hand. Jack put the papers down and stood up. Tilly stopped what she doing and looked over to Rachel as she finished the conversation on the phone.

"Mum's in hospital, Jack. Her home help found her. She's had a heart attack," her voice was quiet, withdrawn and shocked.

It seemed to take many empty, silent, uncomfortable hours for the taxi to arrive. Rachel and Jack filed out of the flat in silence like bereaved relatives leaving for a funeral. Tilly stayed at the flat while they went to the hospital. She watched them drive off down the road and then slowly returned to the living room and the task of rolling her joint. She took herself out to the back door and sat on the steps to smoke it. She felt their sadness and did not enjoy getting high at all; she felt guilty, dirty and worthless.

An understanding nurse escorted Rachel and Jack into the ward where their mother was resting. She had tubes from her arms and wires from various points on her chest as a monitor beside the bed beeped in time with her heart rate. A doctor was reading her notes. Sally had her eyes closed and looked pale and peaceful. Rachel sat beside the bed and began to weep softly. Jack stood behind her and stared without any signs of emotion.

"She's stable at the moment, but it was a very close thing. You need to understand that your mother has suffered a serious heart attack. Considering her general health, the time between being discovered and the attack, this will be a very long and complicated healing process for her. There is a very real chance that she may lose the battle," he paused to allow for a response of some kind but got none, "all we can do is wait and monitor her condition," continued the doctor quietly.

"Please rest assured that we are doing all we can for her," he added, curious as to why there were no questions, any shrugs or facial changes. It was almost as if he was not there at all and they could not hear him speak.

"I shall leave you alone for a while. If you need me, I'll be in my office over there," he pointed to a door in the hall but neither Rachel or Jack paid him any attention.

"Can she hear us?" asked Rachel quietly as he was leaving.

"Oh yes. She's only sleeping. Although she is very weak."

Jack took a seat on the opposite side of the bed to Rachel, who held onto her mother's fingers and stroked her hand with her thumb. They sat motionless for a long time as they both watched their mother's face. She hardly moved at all. An occasional eye movement beneath the lid and a deep inhalation was all that disturbed her peace. The beeping machine, although very quiet and unobtrusive, became hypnotic and held the two in a trance. Eventually, after what felt like a very long wait, Sally opened her eyes slowly. She blinked heavily a couple of times and then turned her head to look at Jack.

"James?" she rasped, almost inaudibly.

"We're here mum," he replied.

"Take it easy mum. You've had a rough day," whispered Rachel with a smile.

"It was him," she whispered, "on the telly."

Sally's voice trembled with fear. Her eyes rolled in her shadowy sockets and her bottom lip quivered momentarily.

"Your father. On telly."

"Our father?" asked Rachel.

"Who?" asked Jack as he leaned forward.

"Robert," she whispered, "on telly."

Sally began to weep and then cough. Her monitor flashed a red light and the beeping machine quickened its rhythm. In seconds, a nurse had appeared beside the bed and looked at the monitor. She looked at the watch on her lapel and then at Sally.

"Please," she began, "she needs to rest. The tension is not doing her any good."

"That's Peter Johnson, I think," said Rachel across the bed when the nurse had left.

"What is?" asked Jack.

"I reckon Peter Johnson is our dad!"

"I think you've cracked!"

"Seriously, Jack. Peter Johnson used to be Robert Harrison. He changed his name when he was twenty-three."

161

"How do you know that?" asked Jack as he shook his head.

"It's in the biscuit tin. The stuff from the locker? I got it figured out now!" she whispered.

"It was him," whispered Sally again, "your father. On the telly."

Sally's head lolled from one side to the other as if she had not got the strength to control its movements. Her eyes became heavy and she eventually left them closed.

"Who?" whispered Jack forcefully.

"Your father," she replied quietly as she drifted into a delirious sleep, "on the telly."

"Leave her, Jack. We can come back tomorrow, but I'm telling you, it's Peter Johnson!"

* * * * *

Tilly sat and watched the children's television channel for a while as she tried unsuccessfully not to think of how Rachel and Jack must have been feeling. She loved cartoons; especially the computer generated kind, with their fascinating characters and wonderful landscapes. Unfortunately for Tilly, they did not last long and very soon a weak plot that began to unfold in poorly acted children's drama replaced them. She huffed as she pressed the remote control at random until something interesting appeared. She recognised a street that filled the screen for a second between other faces and places but she was changing channels too quickly for her to stop in time. She switched buttons on the remote and hopped back a couple of channels to search for the glimpse of familiarity she thought she had just seen. The local news was showing the town centre as it was earlier and the taped off area where Jonny had been shot. A line of several police officers were walking up and down with their heads bowed looking for clues as a sergeant gave a statement to the news team. He knew the make and model of the car as well as the registration number. Tilly instantly assumed that they should know the driver and if that was the case, then why had they not arrested him? Her suspicion that

Dave was a corrupt police officer crept into her thoughts again but this time it was less believable than it was before, although there was a nagging doubt in the back of her mind. The on-location journalist revealed that one man had been found dead at the scene and another was critically ill in hospital with life threatening gunshot wounds. Neither man had been named as the police thought that this incident was connected to the killing of a young man that had been named as Darren Holmes.

"Popper!" whispered Tilly.

A photo-fit picture of a man wanted in relation to this incident appeared on screen. Tilly recognised the black-and-white sketch as a hit-and-miss match for Tony, the man that had threatened Rachel outside the café.

"Wanker!" she whispered.

Chapter 9

Peter slid the papers he was reading under a leather-bound folder when he heard a knock at the door. He put down his expensive pen and quickly straightened up his desk. He scanned the work surface to make sure he had hidden all traces of whatever it was he was doing and then he rested his hand on the mouse beside the keyboard.

"Come in!"

Peter's personal assistant bowed as she entered and held the door wide for Dave to follow in after her. She nodded her head and then left the room. It was only when the door had clicked shut that Peter stood up and thrust out his hand to Dave. Dave gave him a firm handshake in a tight grip. Peter gestured to a chair and the two men sat opposite each other at Peter's desk. Dave could sense a tension in the room, but not enough to intimidate or concern him.

"You have news?" asked Peter as he made himself a little more comfortable.

"She was looking for her father. Trail went cold and she's dropped it. I think she was satisfied when she found her brother instead. Seems our poor little whore wanted to be a part of a family," Dave tugged at his cufflinks.

"And the brother? Who is he?"

"He's one of the guys from the squat; a harmless junkie! We had a little trouble with one of his friends and he..." he paused and shrugged his shoulders, "...had an accident."

"I saw that boy on the news. So that was your handy work, eh?" Peter questioned with a smile.

Dave looked at Peter in silent thought. He had killed people before; sometimes in self-defence, sometimes for money, but Dave had always been able to justify it to himself one way or another. This time it was different and he was not altogether comfortable with the killing. He was a young man in his prime, not unlike Dave used to be when he was that age. His death was accidental and pointless. He could have been frightened off with a sustained beating but it all went wrong. Dave had lost control of the situation. His regret collected as a lump in his throat, which he coughed out with no further thought before he took a deep breath.

"She's content to stay home now and nurse her junkie brother and alcoholic mother back to full health like a Good Samaritan," he smiled.

"And what of Ms Cooper?" asked Peter, as he rubbed his hands together.

"She's currently taking a long, cold vacation in the high dependency ward at the General. Her health caught up with her."

"So it's over then?" whispered Peter to himself with a growing smile curling across his lips, "She's finished searching and found only her mother and brother. A junkie, an alcoholic and a whore! What an unholy trinity!" he laughed.

Peter felt a weight lift from him. A welcome wave of relief flowed through him with a heavy sigh, releasing the anxiety that had crept into his life ever since he had seen the photo in Rachel's purse. Dave saw his face relax into an expression that said it all. There was no consideration for the affects this had had on the people around him. It was all about Peter, and Dave resented that.

"Carl's been hit. It's serious," interrupted Dave.

Peter stopped smiling and immediately sat upright.

"Shit! We've got a shipment coming over the river tonight and I hoped you and he would collect it for me," Peter looked concerned, but it was not at the fact that Carl was injured.

"Will he make it?" added Peter, hoping to regain some respect.

"Touch and go. We'll know soon enough," Dave's voice was void of emotion. He had lied to Peter so many times that it had become second nature and he had learned to hide his feelings where nobody, especially Peter, could sense them. It was safer that way. Showing emotions was a sign of weakness that his enemies, or even his associates, could exploit. He was outwardly unaffected, although the internalised anger and loss bubbled away beneath the surface and added to the hatred he had been storing up for years. He felt like a well-shaken bottle of champagne ready to burst and he knew that when his cork popped, it would be loud, intense and aimed at Peter.

"Where's the drop?" asked Dave, deliberately changing the subject, not only to avoid talking about it but also to simmer the bubbling tension.

"Victoria Dock, on the back of a legitimate cargo. It works better that way," Peter smiled, "Russian's I think; total novices – they haven't got a clue! My guess is they've accidentally come into a bit of gear and they want to move it on quick!"

Dave nodded. He'd seen this scene before. A lucky cargo, or 'sea gear', as it was known. It was rare, but not unusual, for a ship to come across a discarded cargo either floating on the sea or dredged up in fishing nets. It was usually a sign that a previous ship had been searched, usually short-range trawlers, so the inexperienced crew ditched the illegal cargo over the side to hide the evidence. The only downside to a lucky cargo was the increased chance that it had been tainted or damaged. A lot of money could be wasted on gear with little or no street value if the packaging was not watertight. Dave put it all to the back of his mind. Why should he care anymore? He was getting out of this hell once and for all.

"You coming too? Carl's out of service and it would be too short notice to call in any of the others."

There was a silent moment as Peter got up and walked back and forth behind his desk as he rubbed his chin.

"OK," Peter sounded nervous. He had taken shipments before, in his early days, but he knew it was the most vulnerable part of his business, "are you sure she's off the trail?"

"Forget about her, Peter, she's history!"

* * * * *

Rachel plucked her phone from her bag, raised it to her ear and flipped it open in one single, smooth, movement.

"Hello?"

Lisa began to talk very fast, like an excited schoolgirl on amphetamines. Rachel knew immediately that this meant she had some gossip that she considered 'juicy' and wanted the whole world to hear. Rachel shook her head in silence, not really interested, as Lisa blurted out a long-winded tale about how one of Lisa's friends had been attacked just a few nights ago. The friend had not reported the incident to the police because of who the attacker was, but she was telling all of her girlfriends exactly what he had done to her. Now Rachel was getting the story too, blow by gruesome blow. Rachel knew that Lisa had a tendency to exaggerate the truth somewhat when it came to reciting stories that she had heard on the grapevine. She listened intently and tried to shed away the layers of sensationalism and remember that there may be an element of truth somewhere.

"OK, OK! Lisa!" Rachel snapped into the phone in order to stop her friend talking for a moment, "Why are you telling me?"

"Because the bastard that did it is the rich bloke we pulled the other night! The one that couldn't handle us both? Remember? The lottery winner!"

Rachel's jaw dropped and her eyes widened in shock. She could not believe what she was hearing. She began to pace up and down her living room as she became very interested in what Lisa had to tell her.

"Peter Johnson? Are you sure?"

"I knew you wouldn't believe it!" squealed Lisa, "but I guarantee - its true!"

Rachel double-checked the details and asked enough questions to ensure that she was absolutely convinced of what Lisa claimed had really happened.

"Listen, Lisa. This is more serious than you could ever imagine! Get round to mine as soon as you can! This is big – very big!" Rachel stood still behind her couch with one hand on her hip.

"Sorry, babe, no can do; I've a client due in an hour," she replied disappointed.

"Believe me Lisa, there is nothing more important than this right now! Rearrange the client!"

"Rachel! You know something? Please tell!" replied the squeaking Lisa.

Rachel paced again as she spoke into the phone. She gesticulated with her free hand and her voice grew louder and sterner.

"Seriously, Lisa, no client is worth missing this! Get here now!" Rachel hung up and dropped the phone onto her couch.

Lisa stared at her phone with a furrowed brow and a down-turned mouth.

"Bitch hung up on me!" she whispered.

* * * * *

When Lisa arrived at Rachel's flat, Tilly ushered her in quickly. Curiously, Tilly stepped out onto the doorstep and looked both ways down the street. She closed the door and turned the key in the lock. With a short, sharp squeak that made Lisa wince, she slid a small brass bolt into place at the bottom of the door. Lisa, feeling slightly nervous, asked politely,

"Who are you?"

"Tilly. Friend of Rachel's."

Lisa looked her up and down and frowned slightly as Tilly skipped passed her into the living room.

"Poured you one already, honey," Rachel said as she pointed to a steaming mug of coffee, "Make yourself at home."

Rachel introduced Tilly and Jack to Lisa and began to explain how they had all met. She told her about her search for her mother, some of which Lisa already knew from previous conversations, but the last time they spoke, Sally was still unknown and Lisa had doubted that she would ever be found. Jack was welcome news to them both. Rachel made eye contact with him when she began to tell his story and smiled a broad, happy smile that shone through her brilliant green eyes. Jack returned the smile with an equal amount of genuine happiness. Lisa looked him in the eye as Rachel described how they came to find each other. She admired him discreetly from behind her mug and thought he would be a handsome young man if he cleaned himself up a bit. Though try as she might, she could not see any similarity to Rachel in his features at all. The way he smiled back to Rachel obviously held a lot of affection for her. Lisa thought it sweet, and felt warm inside. Rachel spoke of Popper with sadness in her voice that brought a lump to Jack's throat and caused Tilly to weep. Lisa was engrossed in the adventure and held her mug so tight she thought it might break. Rachel told the story with such commitment and feeling that Lisa too felt emotional. She went on to talk about Peter Johnson and her family ties. She explained about her mother and Neil and how Peter had caused his death. Lisa listened for the most part in a silence broken only by an occasional "ah" or "what?" and "No!" When the story had been laid out at Lisa's feet, she sat back in her chair and breathed a heavy sigh. Jack, Tilly and Rachel also took a deep breath, and almost in unison, sipped their drinks.

"This is big!" Lisa agreed.

Tilly nodded quietly to herself.

"Fuckin' huge!" Jack sighed.

He only now truly appreciated the length and depth of the situation as he had heard it all in context. He had sat and listened to the whole story as if Rachel were talking about someone else, not Jack and his friends. The objective view gave him a different perspective and he sympathised with his own character in the narrative. He had become so absorbed in the story that he had seen it play out in his mind's eye and had lost sight of his immediate surroundings. He shook his head and tried to focus on the moment.

"I need you to get your friend here too," said Rachel in a very matter-of-fact voice as she nodded, "we have a lot of work to do."

* * * * *

Dave met Peter at his office as they had arranged. All the staff had gone home, except two cleaners, one of which diligently emptied the bins while the other pushed a vacuum cleaner in-between the desks in the outer office. They shouted a broken conversation about the darts team in their local pub and paid no attention to anything else. Dave and Peter were just starting the pleasantries when Peter's mobile phone rung out from his jacket pocket.

"Give me two minutes," said Peter as he lifted out his phone and then skipped out through the door.

Dave sneaked over to the door and peered out of the tall, thin window in the partition wall. Peter walked away from the office with his back to him. From inside of his overcoat, cleverly concealed, Dave took a large brown envelope and carefully tucked it under a pile of post in Peter's 'In' tray. He went back to the window and checked to see where the cleaners were and to make sure Peter was out of earshot. Satisfied he was alone for while, he flipped open his phone and tapped at the buttons as he wrote a text message. Dave had only just slipped his phone back into his pocket when Peter popped his arrogant smiling face around the door.

"OK?" he said.

Dave drove. Peter fidgeted nervously all the way to the docks. He bit his nails as he mumbled his anxieties to Dave, who paid them no attention. As they neared the docks, they turned off the main road and onto a rough surfaced drive, which quickly diminished and became little more than an orderly scattering of gravel. The noise of travelling on such a surface added to the tension growing in Peter's ears. He shook his head and cleared his throat. The air was full of the sounds of the docks; water lapping against the lock gates and seagulls that filled the grey and orange sky with their calls. The smell of fresh fish and stale diesel was in the air and it clung to the back of Peter's throat like a sticky gum. Beyond the lock gates a little further down the dock, a red and silver metallic ship gleamed in the last few rays of the setting sun. A garage-sized door was open in the side of the boat and a broad runway rested between it and the dock. A large crane loomed unmanned and motionless on giant metal legs like an alien vessel, foreboding and intimidating. Large containers, piled carefully in a holding bay, restricted the view beyond the crane and several more were stacked on the deck of the boat.

Peter got out of the car and stood by his door. Dave walked over to the edge of the dock and looked down into the water. The exposed seaweed and clinging barnacles beneath the high tide line filled the air with the distinctive odour of the sea, fouled with industry and fumes.

"Tides out," he said flatly.

Peter just nodded and folded his arms. He scanned the horizon for any signs of life. Dave walked over towards the doorway. He appeared to be very relaxed and unconcerned by the unfamiliar surroundings and the potentially dangerous situation he was about to enter into.

"Get the cash. Wait by the car," Peter ordered.

Dave walked back to the car and lifted the boot. He took out a green suitcase and stood by the driver's side door. A man in heavy black clothing appeared from the opening in the side of the boat, pulling behind him a low-loading trolley with two stout plastic boxes piled on it. Peter began to walk towards the man, slowly at first and then he quickened his pace. Dave waited by the car with his arms folded and the suitcase at his feet in front of him.

"Iss yours?" said the man in what Dave assumed to be a Russian accent.

Peter looked at the two plastic boxes. They looked sea-stained and slightly battered. It was, as he had suspected, a lucky cargo. He noticed that the side of the box had taken a severe scraping which may have breached the watertight integrity of the sealed unit.

"Open it!" demanded Peter as he mimed opening the box.

The Russian lifted the lid on the top box to reveal a row of very carefully aligned plastic bags full of white powder. The bags were clean and unbroken. The inside of the box was flawless and dry, with no sign of water damage.

"A thing of beauty…" whispered Peter.

"You pay now!" snapped the man.

Peter looked at the Russian and tilted his head slightly. The man stood up and raised himself to his full height, which was still considerably shorter than Peter, but he looked very proud. He too tilted his head and then pointed over to the stacked containers. Peter looked over and saw a man with his back to a crate and a gun at his shoulder pointed straight at Peter. The Russian nodded and tilted his head the other way. He pointed up toward the deck of the boat where another man also pointed a gun.

"OK!" nodded Peter and he turned to beckon Dave.

Dave picked up the suitcase and walked over carefully. He scrutinised the man by the containers and the second up on the deck. He thought about his pistol in his inside pocket; if he could get to it quick enough, would it outsmart both gunmen? He did not know. Part of him did not care. He measured up the distances and calculated the effective range of the rifles and his own weapon. He did not like the odds he gave for the likelihood of this deal turning sour and everything getting loud and deadly. He stood beside Peter and looked down into the box.

"Well, I know you're out of practice, but you think you should check it first?" suggested Dave as he offered Peter a small pocketknife.

Peter looked at Dave with a frown and then at the powder. He picked up a bag from the box and pierced it with the knife. He pulled it out slowly to make sure he had a small sample of powder resting on the blade. He licked the end of the knife and reluctantly swallowed the powder. He smacked his lips, nodded, gently squeezed the bag in his hand a couple of times and the returned it to its companions in the box.

"Pay the man!" he demanded quickly.

Dave offered the green suitcase and the Russian almost snatched it from his grip. He then took the trolley by the handles. He turned to leave as the Russian began to unzip the case. Peter quickened his pace and got to the car long before Dave had managed to drag the trolley over the uneven surface beneath the rickety wheels. As they opened the door, they heard a loud shout ring out as the window in the passenger side door instantly shattered with a dull crackling pop. Dave dropped the handles of the trolley and reached inside his coat. He pulled out his gun and fired two shots. The gunman fell back onto the containers with a thud and then hit the ground with a groan. Another shot came from the deck of the boat and harmlessly hit the ground a few feet to Dave's right sending dust flying up at an angle. Dave was at a disadvantage; the sniper had the higher ground and he had ducked out of sight. He ran toward the car and sat with his back to the door. The gunman had ducked out of sight. In the moment of safety, he reached out for the trolley and pulled it closer to him. It provided a little cover, but nowhere near enough to keep him safe from the sniper's bullets. A black outline appeared and another shot sounded. Dave heard the bullet whistle passed his ear and pierce the bodywork of the car behind him. He felt the heat as the metal tore open.

"Sweet mother of God!" he growled through gritted teeth.

Dave could see a hint of silhouette against the skyline of the boat and aimed several shots at it. They whistled as they ricocheted off the metal bodywork. Peter had got inside the car and pushed the door open for Dave. He jumped in headfirst and quickly turned round to grab the top box from the trolley. He threw it onto the back seat and then reached out for the next box. Peter had already slammed the car in reverse and Dave could not get a proper grip on the box although the open door scooped it up as they drove passed. The lid flipped open and several bags fell out onto the road. They instantly split and spilled white powder across the gravel as small wisps of white clouds puffed into the air. Another bullet shattered the windscreen and embedded in the seat beside Peter.

"Shit!"

He swung the car round in a skid, slammed it into gear and pushed his foot down hard. They screeched their way over the rough ground in a cloud of dust and a hail of bullets. The plastic box, trapped beneath the car, rolled noisily against the gravel. The car bumped and the plastic buckled. Bags of white powder burst and splashed along the gravel as the car sped off. Eventually, battered and crushed, the box bounced out from beneath the car and rolled over the quayside into the dock, taking the few remaining bags with it.

"Bloody Russians!" whispered Peter.

"What the hell happened there?" asked Dave, suspiciously.

"Oldest trick in the book! I put one layer of money over a pile of scrap paper. It looked convincing at first glance but he obviously lifted the top layer!"

Dave shook his head and felt his anger grow.

"That's such a novice trick! Any fool would know that one!" Dave whispered angrily.

He looked over to the back seat and saw the box. He noticed out of the rear window that the Russian in black had joined the gunfight using the rifle that the man by the crates had dropped.

"They will come after you!" warned Dave.

"No they won't!" Peter smiled, "This whole deal has been under a false name! They have been dealing with a dealer that does not exist!"

Suddenly, another bullet whistled into the car and embedded itself in the back seat.

"No papers, no cheques, no banks, just cash."

Another bullet took out the rear light with a loud pop. More bullets continued to embed themselves at random into the car as they sped away from the sniper.

"They're amateurs and deserve to be taken for all they've got!" Peter sounded so confident that he had completed his devious task without any chance of reprisals.

The gunshots had ceased. They had driven out of range and the Russians had no transport to give chase. Peter assumed he was home free. Dave was not so sure and shook his head. He felt his phone vibrate in his pocket.

* * * * *

Rachel and Lisa had gone out to the Masonic Lodge to meet with Claire after her shift. Jack and Tilly stayed home. Tilly rolled a joint in the living room while Jack prepared something to eat. She joined him in the kitchen when she had finished and watched him while he buttered the toast and then scooped the eggs from the boiling water. He exaggerated his movements as he mimicked a celebrity chef playing for the camera on a prime-time cookery show.

"It's a classic dish!" he said in a forced accent, "Beans a la toast et un poached egg!" he smiled as he plated two portions of steaming food.

Tilly laughed and took a plate off him. They returned to the living room and sat down to eat in front of the television. They hopped through several channels until they found something they could both enjoy. Tilly had not felt as settled for a long time. She felt warmth; not just in the room around her and in the food, which was a blessing when she considered some of the living standards she had endured, but because she felt respected. Finally, after a lifetime of rejection, she felt wanted and that made her feel good about herself. Jack looked at her in silence as they ate their first sumptuous mouthful. When Tilly looked up and their gazes met, he smiled a smile that said "me too".

* * * * *

Lisa comforted Claire as she openly wept her story to Rachel in shocking detail. Every line made her more and more determined to put Peter Johnson behind bars. When Claire finished, there was a short silence and a few comforting gestures from all three damp-eyed women to each other. There was a unity, a sisterhood, an unspoken bond that told each of them that they all understood; they all felt the pain. Rachel explained that she had evidence that could end Peter's false life and put him in the dock to answer to his crimes, but she could sense a growing need for retribution. Lisa nodded in anger at the thought of justice. Claire smiled through her tears at the thought of satisfying revenge. Rachel tried to emphasise the need for them to remain within the law. She insisted that they did not act as low as he did, for this would make them his equal and they all knew that they were worth more than he was. Rachel repeated herself, trying to convince her friends and trying to convince herself. There was a moment of silent reflection, broken suddenly when Claire remembered the journalist and began to explain about her encounter with her in the ladies toilets.

"She said she got some photo's of him threatening me," explained Claire as she recalled the conversation as best as she could, "but we kind of had a fight! Well, a shove at least," she added.

She explained that even though they had parted in anger, she had found her business card left out on the bar with the scribbled message that she should contact her if she needed to. Rachel insisted that the journalist must join them in their plotting and Lisa immediately agreed.

"She could be very useful," she nodded thoughtfully, "if all else fails we can sell your story to the press and his reputation will be shattered if nothing else. I bet you're not the only victim he's had!" she added.

"And a journalist should do that quite nicely," added Rachel.

"Especially with photos," nodded Claire.

Claire rummaged in her handbag and retrieved her purse. She slid out a business card and held it aloft for all to see.

"I knew I had it on me," she said.

Claire tapped the number into her phone and within a minute she was in full conversation with the journalist. Claire fed her enough information to let her know that she had a seriously delicious story but not enough to satiate her appetite over the phone. She arranged to meet her at the Masonic Lodge at seven on Friday, at which time she would explain everything in full glorious colour, with no detail left unexplored.

"Oh, and don't forget, Julie, bring your photographer. He would like to see this," she nodded, "and a video camera," she added quickly as the idea suddenly popped into her thoughts.

* * * * *

Dave and Peter sat in the car behind a row of shops. The street was short and narrow with only one way in and one way out. They sat without talking. Peter looked at the numerous small cubes of glass splashed all over the inside the car. The last few remaining fragments of windscreen clung to the rubber strip along the seam as they gently swayed in the breeze. The leather of the seats had numerous punctures and the stuffing had exploded out of the small holes like singed popcorn. Peter checked his arms and legs to make sure that his expensive suit had not suffered any damage. Reassured, he was surprised to have got off without an injury when he realised how many shots had been fired at them.

Dave breathed a heavy sigh and looked down at his cold gun, empty of bullets. It was only a matter of time before the police traced the shells. Discreetly, he wiped it with a handkerchief and slipped it into his pocket before he sighed again and looked out of the window. The glass was absent and the paintwork scratched. He remembered the sound of the bullet as it whistled passed his ear. The dull thud of the impact as it embedded itself in the door. He leaned out of the window and looked at the hole then turned his attention to the inside of the door and looked for an exit hole. There was nothing. The bullet must have been somewhere inside the bodywork.

"Back to the ranch, Kimosabe!" Peter sighed.

The excitement of the shooting and the swift drive to escape was so invigorating for Peter, but like any good rush, the crash had begun and now he felt a slight depression looming in like a dull wet Sunday afternoon. Dave drove carefully through the town towards Peter's office building. It was late evening and there was nobody about. Dave looked up at the lampposts to see how many CCTV cameras had tracked his broken progress through the deserted streets and raised his eyebrows at the thought of the police officer watching the monitor at that same moment. He parked the shattered car in the staff car park, not easily seen from the main thoroughfare. Dave locked the car with the electronic key fob, paused for a moment of realisation and laughed privately. Four of the windows had been shot through. The passenger side was punctured with bullet holes and two of the lights had been smashed.

"We got hit more than I thought!" he whispered to himself.

"If that were my car, I'd be really pissed off!" laughed Peter, with an arrogant smile.

Dave grumbled and shrugged his shoulders. The signs of the gunfight triggered many morbid thoughts. He wondered how Carl was doing. He had not thought about contacting the hospital since it happened. For the first time he considered his own mortality and felt relieved to be alive. He took the gun from his pocket and looked at it for a moment, then raised the sight to Peter walking away in the distance. He frowned and then slid the gun away inside his jacket. He took one last long look at the car and then turned to the entrance of the Johnson Building. Peter was already in his office with the box open and had started to count the bags of coke by the time Dave had caught up with him. He was piling them up next to the box and smiling to himself.

"I reckon that's about six kilos, what about you?" asked Peter without looking up at Dave.

"Give or take," said Dave with a shrug of his shoulders.

"Well over a quarter of a million! And to think, I paid less than ten grand!" Peter laughed to himself.

"Listen, Peter, I don't want to spoil your fun. You play with your new toy for a while but I'm going to catch up with Carl. See you tomorrow."

"Yeah, yeah, whatever..." Peter said, without looking up from his valuable haul.

Dave took the gun carefully from his pocket and slipped it unnoticed on to the desk next to the gear. He stood outside the office for a moment with his back to the door and listened to Peter laughing and talking to himself.

"What a wanker!" he whispered to himself as he wandered off.

He heard the door open behind him and he stopped in his tracks. He turned around slowly.

"You're going to need a new car!" shouted Peter from the office behind him. He threw a bunch of keys over the desks and Dave stepped forward to catch them.

"Thanks!" he said without any sign of genuine gratitude.

He took the keys in his hand and looked at the enamel BMW logo on the fob. When Dave got downstairs to the car park, he noticed that there were only two cars remaining. One of them was his battered Jaguar with its scratched paint, smashed windows and bullet holes, parked against the wall. The other was a metallic blue BMW parked nearer the entrance. Dave pressed the key fob and the lights flashed back him. He smiled half-heartedly and made himself comfortable in the driver's seat. In next to no time he was pulling up outside the hospital and collecting his pay and display parking ticket.

Chapter 10

Peter knew the photograph. Although he did not want to, he remembered it well. Even though the ink had faded over time and his face looked younger, he recognised himself immediately. He felt hollow. The photo, in amongst his regular post in a plain envelope, had been addressed but not postmarked. It must have been hand delivered through the internal post. At first he thought that the deliverer must have had access to his office but then when he considered that there were several employees across his buildings he concluded that it could have come form anywhere. He shook his head as he stared at the faces on the picture. It was the second man that he was swapping cases with that bothered him. He was known as Boulder, but contrary to his bulky name, he was a short, unassuming character, although he used to run half the criminal industry in Stratford. His merciless acts of violence against his enemies had elevated him to the highest position in the criminal underworld in his district. He was a feared man, with strong links to local crime lords and the Inter City Firm back in the day. Peter still shuddered to think of him, even though he believed he was dead.

He felt the black-and-white past leap from the paper and swell over him like the seventh wave upon the beach, creeping in that little bit further than all other waves before it. His thoughts and feelings flew back to the time in the photograph, he felt scared, small and insignificant, just as he did when he handed that case to Boulder. It was an early rung on a long ladder for Peter. He stepped up as a naive young man and climbed on to become a shrewd and cruel businessman. He never reached the same dizzy heights as Boulder had, but he was catching him fast. Even so, Boulder could still fill Peter's soul with dread and respect from far away and long ago. He thought he had swept away his past and buried it deep enough to be beyond reach. Thinking quickly, he recalled the names of the more powerful people that he had worked with in his early career. He remembered the old acquaintances that he assumed would have the wherewithal to get this picture to him. He mentally listed the suspects that would have the motive and the audacity to be threatening him after all these years.

Somebody had scribbled on the back of the print that he or she wanted to meet with Robert Harrison to discuss the event captured in the photograph. Such a threatening statement stirred up nervousness and nausea in the soulless pits of his gut. His anger grew and he slammed his fist down on the table with a loud growling scream. There was a gentle knock at the door,

"Are you OK, Mr Johnson?" the meek voice from outside questioned.

Peter could see the crinkled outline of his personal assistant showing through the tall windows beside the door.

"Fine, I'm fine."

The assistant stood outside the door with her head bowed, waited for a moment before she walked back to her desk and returned to her administrative tasks. Peter turned his attention back to the picture and tried to deduce who could be attempting to blackmail him. The only clue was Boulder, but he could not remember if he had had any dealings with Peter before he changed his name. It had to be someone that had known him for a long time. The only suspects he could think of were dead. He shook his head and thought hard. Peter felt sure that nobody that knew him as Robert Harrison was still around now.

* * * * *

Rachel and Tilly sat in the kitchen laughing at Jack's dreadful singing as he enjoyed his shower. They waited patiently for Claire and Lisa to arrive. Rachel offered them a room but they decided to go home together in the early hours of the morning. None of them had had much sleep and they were all feeling tired, except Tilly, who was her usual yo-yo self and bounced between being seriously contemplative one moment and humorously childlike the next. Rachel had a headache that she could not shift and she had already maxed out on paracetamol for the morning. Tilly had taken to miming the words to the song that Jack was destroying in his own discordant way. She was gesticulating with her arms as if she were a passionate singer. Rachel wished she could laugh but her tired body and sleep-deprived mind would not allow her to do it. Despite everything, Tilly kept her humour. It was as if nothing else mattered to Tilly. She was an eternal optimist with a love for life untouched by any multitude of problems her existence may throw at her. Rachel admired her positivity.

There was a knock at the door and Tilly sprang off like a startled animal ducking for cover. She was out of the kitchen, through the hall and peering out of the window in the door before Rachel had time to put her drink down and leave the kitchen. Tilly ushered Claire and Lisa in with a comical, majestic bow. Jack came into the living room with a towel wrapped around his waist and another smaller one in his hand. He rubbed his hair and hummed the remaining verse of his song. Claire looked at him and raised an eyebrow with a nod. Jack smiled flirtingly. Tilly giggled and reached out to grab the towel from around his waist. She almost caught it when Jack jumped back and escaped her reach. She giggled again and chased him through the hall, out of sight of the visitors and into a room behind a slammed door. Rachel shrugged her shoulders with a smile and made everyone drinks. They spoke and drank in the living room until Jack and Tilly came through a few minutes later, still laughing. Rachel focussed the gathered friends on the task in hand and the laughing ceased. They all knew why they were meeting and they all understood the importance of what they were about to do.

* * * * *

Peter entered the Grand Hall of the Masonic Lodge in anticipation with a slight fluttering of nervousness in the pit of his stomach. It was a feeling he had not encountered for many years and he was unaccustomed to it. His mind was so tense that he could not concentrate enough to gather his thoughts as efficiently as he would have liked. He could not read the psychological processes behind the activity around him and his usually sharpened senses were somewhat dulled. The Lodge had begun to get busy as small gatherings greeted each other in the aisles and settled at tables. He quickly scanned the room and saw that Dave had already made himself comfortable at one of the tables near the bar. He adjusted his jacket and walked slowly through the Hall, anxiously aware of several pairs of eyes locked onto his every move. Peter knew that people always watched him enter a room; his wealth and good looks ensured that wherever he went he was noticed but this time he was shrouded in paranoia. He looked around discreetly at the onlookers and tried to recognise faces but to no avail. He took a seat opposite Dave.

"Thanks, Dave. I'm glad you could make it," he stated with forced appreciation.

"No worries," replied Dave nonchalantly.

Peter shuffled in his seat and felt very uncomfortable. He did not like having his back to a large room full of people and suggested to Dave that they take another seat nearer the wall.

"You OK? You never said what we were doing here," said Dave.

"I just need you to watch my back for the evening and follow my lead if things get edgy. I'm not entirely sure myself, to be honest Dave, but this could get messy and I might need you," he explained sincerely with a hint of humbleness.

Dave had never seen Peter this vulnerable before. In the early days, Peter had often crumbled under the stress of aggression, the expectations of his peers and pressure from his enemies, but those days had long since passed. Peter had been elevated to an untouchable status and was out of reach, even to the police it would seem. Peter was out of practice and had forgotten what it felt like to be under threat. Dave smiled to himself discreetly as he sipped his wine. Peter stood up slowly and led the way to a side table. He sat with his back to the wall so he could survey the room. The rising tension far outweighed the little security the seating offered. A waitress appeared at the table, standing equidistant between Peter and Dave, with a bottle of over-priced wine in a decorative silver ice bucket. She bowed her head politely in Dave's direction and then turned and smiled at Peter. Peter was about to smile back when he suddenly realised that the waitress was the girl who had accused him of rape and caused a scene at his private function in the presence of an important councillor. She turned and left without saying a word before Peter could say or do anything. He was about to call out after the waitress when Dave interrupted him,

"You sure you're OK?" asked Dave.

"Its nothing," lied Peter as he tried to convince himself that his seeing the waitress was a coincidence.

He sighed loudly and reached for the wine. Peter poured two glasses and then immediately became suspicious. He lifted his glass to the light and peered through the tinted fluid. He turned the bottle in his other hand and scrutinised the contents.

"What's up?" asked Dave.

"Just looking," replied Peter nervously as he replaced the wine in amongst the ice.

Peter checked his watch and gulped down the wine in one draught. He poured another and swallowed half of it before he rested his glass on the table. After a few moments in silence, Dave stood up to leave.

"Excuse me for a minute," he nodded, "too much wine!"

Dave meandered through the ever-increasing gathering towards the toilets. Peter shivered and loosened his tie. He looked at his watch again. He sat for a few minutes allowing his gaze to flit from face to face across the room. Now and again he thought he recognised some of the people and had to look twice to confirm he was mistaken. The faces of the strangers around him mysteriously altered to those of old acquaintances, dead and gone like ghostly reminders from a Dickensian plot. Peter tried to shake his paranoia from his mind but he could not relax. He gulped a glass of wine quickly and poured himself another. Dave stood by the bar, talking to somebody but Peter could not see. A young couple deep in conversation obstructed his view. He leaned over to get a better look just as Dave turned towards him and strode over. He gently held the young woman by the waist as he squeezed passed her. She smiled up at him, flirtingly. Her partner shook his head when she returned her attention to him and the two engaged in a quiet, mild argument.

Dave adjusted his collar and cuffs before he took his seat opposite Peter.

"Time to go," said Peter with a sigh.

"Where?" asked Dave.

"Room 24. Just follow my lead."

Peter swallowed the remainder of his wine as he stood up quickly and became light-headed. He stood motionless for a moment, trapped in a heightening dizzy spell. He concentrated on breathing slowly and deeply until he regained his balance and felt confident that the whirl had passed. Curiously amused by the change in Peter's character, Dave looked on. Peter led the way to the lift and paused outside the doors expectantly. Dave instinctively stepped forward and pressed the button to summon the lift. With a subtle ping and a green light, the lift arrived and the doors slid open. Annelise was standing in the lift with a silver tray. She gasped in shock when she saw Peter and walked out of the lift quickly. She gave him a wide berth with a worried look on her face as she quickly went on her way. Peter watched her trotting down the corridor and shook his head. He paused thoughtfully and then stepped into the lift. Dave pressed the button on the panel and the two men stood bold like mobsters in a silent film as the lift ascended. Peter waited in the lift after the door had opened and appeared a little reluctant to leave the small sanctuary. Dave paused in the corridor and stared back at Peter. He was looking down at his feet with his hands clasped in front of him, like an altar boy saying his prayers.

"You coming?" asked Dave.

Peter looked up, took a deep breath and then stepped out of the lift. He adjusted his tie and straightened his jacket as he walked down the corridor two strides ahead of Dave. When he reached the door, he paused again.

"Keep your wits about you. Follow my lead," he whispered flatly without looking at Dave.

Dave nodded slowly and smiled to himself. Peter raised his hand to knock at the door and then decided against the idea. He placed his hand on the knob, twisted it firmly and pushed the door slowly. He stepped into the room with his eyes closed, not knowing what to expect. His stomach turned and he felt nauseous. The wine in his stomach seemed to be burning its way up through his chest. He stood just inside the door and waited for a few seconds with his eyes closed. When he opened them, there was nobody there. Dave stepped in behind Peter and closed the door. He twisted the lock in the centre of the knob to the 'locked' position without Peter noticing. He stood against the door with his arms folded across his chest.

Peter walked slowly into the room. A pair of ceiling-to-floor curtains, drawn closed, covered the far wall, and the white sofa in front of them was scattered decoratively with cushions in various shades of brown. There was a rectangular coffee table in front of the sofa, covered in papers and photographs, with a large white fur rug beneath it. There were two doors to the left and one to the right, all closed. Against the wall to the right was a large unit with glass shelves, adorned with simple, stylish ornaments. There was a tall up lighter in the far corner in front of a bookshelf offering the only illumination. Behind him and to his left there was a small wooden unit with a television on it. The room was unthreatening. There was nothing unusual or intimidating about it at all. Peter stopped in the centre of the room,

"Hello?" he said boldly.

He looked down at the table and saw photographs of himself, taken many years ago, handing a briefcase to Boulder. He immediately recognised them as being from a series taken on the same day as the one he had found in his post. He scanned the papers and saw his change of name deed, several tax returns and few letters under the name of Robert Harrison. The atmosphere of the room suddenly twisted on its axis and Peter felt afraid. His haunting past crept into his psyche with sharp, razor-like claws and ear-piercing echoes.

"Boulder?" he asked out loud with his voice trembling nervously.

Dave shook his head slowly and looked down at the floor to hide his growing smile. He felt apprehensive as he shuffled his feet a little. The sound attracted Peter's attention.

"What the hell's going on, Dave?"

He stared at Dave and for a brief moment he saw a flashing something around Dave's head, almost like a ghostly blue halo. He shook his head and looked again. It had gone. His arms and legs were beginning to feel light and empty, as if filled with helium. Just then, he heard a door open quietly and turned round to see Rachel arm-in-arm with Lisa.

"Hello," they said in unison, with wide smiles.

Their voices seemed to emanate towards Peter in stereo. They both walked over to the sofa and sat down.

"You?" exclaimed Peter, puzzled. He was beginning to doubt his senses and suspected that somebody had tampered with the wine he drank earlier.

"Hello Daddy!" smiled Rachel.

The words hit Peter like a demolition ball. He remembered the photograph in her purse on the night he first met Rachel and Lisa. The haunting image had stayed in his mind and taunted him in his secret moments when his memory toyed with his thoughts. He believed she had given up the search and was no longer interested in who her father was.

"How are you feeling?" Rachel asked.

Rachel sounded strong and confident although inside she was scared. Lisa felt nervous and fidgeted a little in her seat. Peter began to feel less threatened as he realised who was behind this plan to blackmail him. He turned to Dave and shrugged his shoulders. Dave smiled and tilted his head. As Peter turned to face the girls, he smiled smugly.

"What the hell do you little girls think you're playing at?" he scolded, "Do you know who you're dealing with here?"

"Peter Johnson," started Rachel in her rebellious tone, "previously known as Robert Harrison. Murderer, rapist and drug dealing scum!"

Rachel stood up as she finished her sentence and looked Peter straight in the eye. Shocked into silence, he began to feel slightly dizzy and wondered why. He remembered the wine. He thought about the faces downstairs and the waitress.

"What have you done to me?" he asked.

"What have *we* done? *We*?" scorned Rachel; "*We* have done nothing. This is all down to *you*. You must have known that sooner or later your dirty little secrets would come back to bite your arse," Rachel reached down for the papers on the table.

"Everything you have done is here in black and white!" she stated as she held up various sheets in front of him, "except of course my mother, who is feeling a lot better now, thanks for asking,"

Rachel held up a sheet of paper at a time and let it drift slowly to the floor as she released it from her grip.

"And poor Neil," she continued angrily, "let's not forget Neil, shall we?"

"What about him?" Peter was shocked that she knew but then he quickly concluded that Sally must have told her everything, "No proof!" he added flatly as he rubbed the back of his neck.

"But you drowned him didn't you? You couldn't bear to lose Sally. Or was it because you just couldn't bear to lose?"

"He deserved it. Nobody cheats me!" Peter snarled.

The voices in the room echoed around him and his vision had changed. Perspective was different somehow and nothing in the room seemed to be still anymore. Everything seemed to be vibrating slowly and changing shades.

"Feeling OK?" smiled Rachel.

"What have you done?" he said slowly from behind gritted teeth.

"Same as you did to Neil. Remember?"

He took a step forward towards the girls and Lisa instinctively stood up. Peter saw traces of Lisa behind her as they stood up and created a visual echo that only Peter could see. She clung to Rachel and stared Peter in the eye.

"You're going down, you bastard!" she snarled.

"You and who's army?" he laughed as he clicked his fingers to Dave.

Dave took a couple of steps forward into the room and reached inside his jacket. He slowly revealed his gun and raised it in front of him.

"Good boy!" whispered Peter, "Now waste these fuckin' whores!" he growled louder as he tried hard to keep a grip on reality. The sounds in the room had become louder and more present. His hands were sweating and his flesh felt damp all over.

Rachel trembled a little and swore under her breath. This was not in the plan. She was lost as she saw her routine slip away from her grasp. Now what could she do?

"This has got his finger prints all over it! I made sure of that," Dave smiled as he threw the gun onto the couch beside Rachel, "and the cops are looking for it!"

Peter was shocked. His jaw dropped. He concentrated hard on the gun as it bounced on the soft furnishing.

"Judas!" he snarled and reached inside his own jacket.

He pulled out his own cold piece and let two shots fly. The world slowed down for Peter and all his movements became fluid. Dave was thrown back with the force of the bullets and they embedded themselves deep within his shoulder and upper arm. His white shirt was quick to redden as he hit the wall behind him and slumped down towards the floor. Lisa screamed as Rachel reached down for the gun. Before she could grab it, Peter fired another bullet that whistled passed Rachel and spat into the back of the couch. She immediately stood upright and still as Lisa held her arm tightly.

"Don't bother!" Peter hissed, desperately trying to hold the gun above the horizontal, but it was becoming very heavy and felt like warm, liquid rubber in his hand.

He swayed on his feet and tried hard to remain upright. He was hallucinating and the dancing lights he could see in the corner of his eye were distracting him. There was a slight sound behind Peter but before he could turn around he felt a sharp pain in the side of his neck.

"Not one move or I squeeze this needle!" whispered Jack.

He had been hiding in the bathroom with Tilly and sneaked out behind Peter as he had been threatening Rachel. He had stealthily sidled up to him and held a loaded syringe in his neck. He grabbed the back of his collar with his free hand and gripped a bundle of shirt and jacket fabric in his tightly clenched fist. The collar was tight against Peter's throat and his breathing was awkwardly restricted. Jack had buried the hypodermic needle up to the chamber.

"This is filthy heroin from your very own supply," continued Jack, "and this needle is one I used earlier! If you're enjoying that acid trip your on, you're gonna love this shit!"

Peter feared to move. Only his eyes flicked around in their sockets as he breathed slowly through his nose. The walls had begun to move slowly as if they were breathing; the floor became as water and rolled like gentle waves on a calm sea. Hideous faces had appeared in the light and dark shades of the furniture and taunted him with beckoning gestures of hatred and threats of death.

"You want to know if I got HIV? Hep?" Jack continued, "It's the waiting after the test that's hardest. Screws you up, all day and night!"

Peter felt his stomach turn as the fear tunnelled deep inside him like a cancerous mole. He felt a cold wave of swaying imbalance as it swept sluggishly over him. The room had taken on a hostile ambience and he felt everything tower over him. He felt small and insignificant, like a cartoon character in an illustrated nightmare.

"Now you drop your little toy there and let the girls leave!" whispered Jack.

He deliberately made his voice sound sinister although he was incredibly nervous and felt as if his acting would not fool anyone. Rachel and Lisa were very convinced. Lisa was so scared now that she had started to cry and Rachel was feeling sick. Peter opened his hand and the gun dropped like lead to the rug. He saw several versions of the same gun fall at slightly different rates, as if time had slipped out of place and the motion carried a visual trace.

"I hope you're prepared to kill me," started Peter with a hollow voice, "because this crap you have here is not worth the paper it's copied on!" Peter pointed slowly towards the table and the paperwork.

"Well, this is where we have the upper hand because if you look closely over there," Jack pointed up to the top corner of the large curtains, "see that little red light?"

The collar around Peter's neck became loose and he could breath freely again. The sense of relief was heightened several-fold by the chemicals in his bloodstream, toying with his senses. He inhaled as deeply as he could through his nose. His chest inflated like a balloon and he thought it would burst. He moved only his eyes and tried his best to keep his neck still. The needle was hot under his flesh, like a burning rod of iron, and he thought he could feel it in his throat.

"So?" Peter was confused. He could see thousands of tiny lights, all different colours in the corner, flickering across the walls and up over the ceiling.

"So you're on telly!" nodded Jack.

Peter tensed unintentionally and shuddered for a second. The needle in his neck snapped. Jack held onto the plastic tube as a small droplet of fluid dripped onto Peter's shoulder. Peter winced as he turned and the needle, still buried in his flesh, burned with a ferocious intensity disproportionate to its actual size. Jack stepped back as Peter reached down for the gun. As he stooped over, Lisa kicked him in the stomach and Peter rolled back onto the floor, away from his target. Rachel reached for the gun on the couch and Lisa, seeing what she doing, pulled Rachel away with a jerk,

"Don't touch that one!"

Peter rolled over in the direction of his own gun, but Jack had already got to it. He stood over Peter and pointed the barrel at his head. Jack was scared that he might pull the trigger unintentionally and loosened his grip a little. He trembled with fear, although he tried not to let it show.

"Don't move a muscle!" he growled.

Peter had lost control of his senses although his mind was still trying to tell him what he should do. His limbs were no longer his own and were beyond his control. Perspective had been lost as light and shade danced all around him. Faces meandered around their own features and the silence between the sounds was distinctly audible.

"OK," shouted Rachel with a trembling voice.

Peter heard a door open and then the faces of Tilly and Julie came into view alongside Rachel and Jack. They looked down at him with demanding eyes, wrapped in fire and loathing. He heard a man's voice from the other side of the room say,

"He's going to be OK, but he needs help quick. Police are on their way."

As Peter drifted helplessly into a world of kaleidoscopic nightmares and an all encompassing echo of sound, he heard the sirens wail outside.

* * * * *

Rachel was delighted to see Sally sat up in bed at the hospital, even though wires still connected her to the machines that pinged in time with her heart rate. She smiled a wide smile and leaned forward to kiss her on the cheek. She gently squeezed her hand and whispered,

"Hello, mum."

Jack followed her in and walked over to the other side of the bed. He kissed her on the forehead and gave her a hug as best he could while she was propped up against her pillows. He felt slightly awkward and Sally knew it, although she fully appreciated the gesture and the obvious difficulty with which he performed it.

"It's all over mum. We got him," whispered Rachel.